WAYNE STINNETT

WEIGH ANCHOR

A JESSE MCDERMITT NOVEL

◆ • ◆ • ◆

Caribbean Adventure Series
Volume 26

DOWN ISLAND PRESS

Copyright © 2023
Published by DOWN ISLAND PRESS, LLC, 2023
Beaufort, SC
Copyright © 2023 by Wayne Stinnett
Library of Congress cataloging-in-publication Data
Stinnett, Wayne
Weigh Anchor/Wayne Stinnett
p. cm. - (A Jesse McDermitt Novel)
ISBN: 978-1-956026-65-8
Cover and graphics by Aurora Publicity
Edited by Marsha Zinberg, The Write Touch
Final Proofreading by Donna Rich
Interior Design by Aurora Publicity
Published by Down Island Press, LLC

If you'd like to receive my newsletter, please sign up on my website. WWW.WAYNESTINNETT.COM.
Once or twice a month, I'll bring you insights into my private life and writing habits, with updates on what I'm working on, special deals I hear about, and new books by other authors that I'm reading.

The Gaspar's Revenge Ship's Store is open.

There, you can purchase all kinds of swag related to my books, and even my books themselves, in whatever format you choose.
You can find it at
WWW.GASPARS-REVENGE.COM

Also by Wayne Stinnett

The Jerry Snyder Caribbean Mystery Series

Wayward Sons   Voudoo Child   Friends of the Devil

The Charity Styles Caribbean Thriller Series

Merciless Charity   Enduring Charity   Elusive Charity
Ruthless Charity   Vigilant Charity   Liable Charity
Reckless Charity   Lost Charity

The Young Jesse McDermitt Tropical Adventure Series

A Seller's Market   Bad Blood

The Jesse McDermitt Caribbean Adventure Series

Fallen Out   Rising Storm
Fallen Palm   Rising Fury   Steady As She Goes
Fallen Hunter   Rising Force   All Ahead Full
Fallen Pride   Rising Charity   Man Overboard
Fallen Mangrove   Rising Water   Cast Off
Fallen King   Rising Spirit   Fish On!
Fallen Honor   Rising Thunder   Weigh Anchor
Fallen Tide   Rising Warrior   Swift and Silent
Fallen Angel   Rising Moon
Fallen Hero   Rising Tide

Rainbows of Collars Motivational Series

Blue Collar to No Collar   No Collar to Tank Top

Sam Hoster

Life is full of challenges and you and your team helped me to get over a really big hurdle. I am forever grateful.

I know why you do what you do, why you push so hard every day, and why you enjoy it so much. You're doing good work, brother.
Stay Strong!

"If you can't fly, then run. If you can't run, then walk. If you can't walk, then crawl. But whatever you do, you have to keep moving forward."
– Martin Luther King Jr.

Jesse's Island

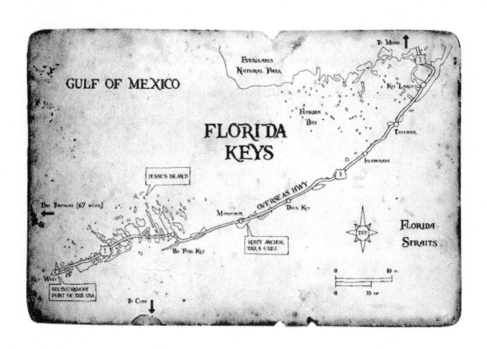

CHAPTER ONE

The old ranch had seen better days. The land itself was unchanged since it had first been settled in 1870, and for centuries before that, transformation only came about due to climate changes. The natural basin had been formed hundreds of millions of years ago, so the 153 years since it had first endured continuous habitation was merely a blink of the eyes of a very old man.

The main house was 150 years old, having replaced the original shack that was built on the land when it was first claimed three years prior. The settler who built both had taken a wife and she wanted a proper home to raise their family. And in 1874, the first child was born in the home—a son.

The sprawling old ranch house had seen six generations born within its walls, and five generations die. The first of each new generation had consistently been born in twenty-five-year intervals, always in the month of November, often very close to a father's or grandfather's birthday. And every single firstborn for 125 years had been a boy.

It stood to reason. Nine months prior was the dead of winter, and in the high, northern basin, those months were exceptionally brutal, with winds howling over 10,000-foot peaks, no matter from which point on the compass they came. When temperatures dropped below zero for weeks on end, there was little else to do to keep warm.

The door opened as a man came out. He slammed it so hard behind him, the glass rattled in the frames. He wore a heavy coat against the early frost and a Western hat on his head. Steam blew from his mouth and nostrils as he looked all around in the crisp morning air.

"Where'd you go this time?" he muttered to himself in a half growl before stepping down off the porch.

He was young, in his mid-twenties. Tall, rangy, and filled with the vigor of youth. Reddish-brown hair hung from under the Stetson he wore and lay loosely on the big white collar of his tan coat.

Stopping in the middle of the front yard, where the grass was beginning to give up its battle with the elements, he turned, looking all around.

Soon, the stark grassland would be covered in several feet of snow, which hid the dangers of cracks and rocks and made travel, even by horseback, a dangerous undertaking. Down in town, there were plows and enough traffic to keep the roads clear, though wet. But in the upper basin, most residents just hunkered in for the winter and made babies.

There was only one out-building—an old barn with a hay loft—but Marshall Grey knew there were four small line shacks on the property's borders, each a half-day's horseback ride from the other. They were situated at the corners of the property, which was roughly square-shaped, and if caught in a blizzard while checking the fence, a rider was only a few hours from one of them.

Grey had already checked the barn and found that her car wasn't there. And the house looked like nobody had been there all night.

He pulled a cell phone from his pocket and checked the bars. Or bar, as it was. Opening his contact list, he scrolled to an entry and tapped it, then held the device to his ear.

"It's Grey," he said. "She's gone again."

CHAPTER TWO

November 1, 2023
Content Keys

There was a cool dryness to the air on the first day of November. The sun was shining, the sky was blue, and there wasn't a cloud in sight.

But I could sense a subtle shift in the weather.

It's often said that if you don't like the weather in South Florida, just wait an hour. But the high-pressure system that had dominated our weather for the last three days was slowly drifting northward, ushering in the typical sub-tropical pattern—hot and humid.

As I finished up the oil change on the Grady-White's Suzuki, I glanced out through the big open doors again.

He was still sitting there.

I'd first noticed him at the end of the dock fifteen minutes earlier. It wasn't like Alberto to sit still for more than the time it took him to wolf down a meal.

I wiped my hands on a shop rag and put the cowl back over the engine, locking it in place. Then I went upstairs to the main part of our stilt house.

"What's with Alberto?" I asked Savannah, as she worked on

sorting and packing all the provisions we'd returned with an hour earlier.

Generally, we liked to stock up enough canned and dry goods to last two weeks, sometimes longer. Meat wasn't much of a concern in the Content Keys.

Our house was in the middle of a high concentration of diverse fish species, many at the top of the list for local restaurant fare, and when it came to shellfish, a lobster dinner was a mere two-hundred-foot swim off the south pier to Harbor Channel. Often, I could get one or two in the rocks right *under* the pier.

Savannah leaned over the sink and looked out the window to the left, where I knew she could see down to the end of the pier.

"He's been sitting there a long time," she said. "Do you think something's troubling him?"

"Guess I'll go down there and find out," I replied, heading toward the door. "Oil's changed in the Suzuki. I'll get to the Yam-a-hammer this afternoon."

"We're going to the dinner concert at the community theater at four. Will you have time to do both?"

I paused halfway through the door and grinned back at her. "Probably not."

"Good thing you don't have any flats charters scheduled for tomorrow, then. The *Yam-a-hammer* can wait."

I closed the door, grinning, and walked over to the steps. It'd been almost four months since Savannah had called me, crying, and asking if it was too late to come home.

It'd then taken another agonizing four days until she and Alberto had returned to our little island.

During that time, we'd talked on the satellite phone for hours every day, running up a huge bill, like a couple of love-sick teenagers, It wasn't until the afternoon of Savannah and Alberto's second day of the long crossing that she told me about what had happened in the Yucatan.

I remembered well the sinking feeling I'd gotten in the pit of my stomach when, in a very strained voice, she'd told me how she'd been forced to give the order to kill a man.

Charity had taken the shot, but it was Savannah's call—a cruel twist of fate.

By then, I'd already gotten a full report from Deuce, forwarded from Paul Bender, one of his field operatives who'd helped Savannah and Charity rescue a kidnapped American girl.

When she'd told me about the shooting in Campeche, she started crying again, vowing that she would be more understanding of the things I'd had to do in the past.

I hadn't been all that sure what she'd meant at the time, but it didn't matter.

I walked down the steps and out onto the pier toward Alberto. He heard me coming and glanced back, quickly pulling the front of his T-shirt up and wiping his eyes.

Was he crying?

"What's up, little man?" I asked, as I got to the end of the pier and looked out over the water.

He was holding something against his chest—a picture.

"Just thinking," he replied.

I sat down next to him, letting my feet dangle in the water, and reached over, gently tugging the picture away.

"I remember this day," I said softly, looking down at a picture of Alberto and Finn on the beach. It was taken in Roatan, Honduras.

There was a pile of empty clam shells in front of them and Finn was looking up at the camera, with his head cocked to one side. "You both got sick from eating too many."

"Yeah..."

"You miss him, don't ya?"

He looked up at me, his dark, expressive eyes beginning to well up again. "I only got to know him for a few years, and we only got back a month before he died."

I pulled him against my side. "I know, son. It's never long enough."

"How come dogs can't live as long as people?"

I remembered reading something once—some story I'd seen online, supposedly from a kid, but it made the greatest sense to me.

"You understand what true loyalty and unconditional love is, right?" He nodded, so I asked him, "How old do you think you were when you first understood that?"

"That's easy," he replied. "The summer you and mom found me in that old boat."

That kinda kicked me in the side a bit. Alberto had been eight years old when Savannah and I had found him drifting in an old wooden dinghy.

"People are born," I said, staring down at Finn's quizzical expression, "and then it takes us years to learn how to live a good life. You know, like loving unconditionally and being loyal to friends and family." I paused and looked down at my young son. "Well, dogs already know all that stuff from the time they first open their eyes. So they don't have to stay as long."

"But I was supposed to take care of him," he said, his voice cracking. "I owed him my life and we went away."

Another unforeseen consequence. Though not directly related, the pain Alberto was feeling about not being there for Finn was the result of my actions.

I pulled him close and held him tight. Savannah had left in early spring, and they'd returned shortly after Independence Day. Finn had recovered completely from his shark-bite wound while they were gone, but he just wasn't the same until they'd returned. By then, I'd learned from the vet who'd treated him that he was dying of cancer and at his age, there was nothing to be done.

"Don't you worry about that," I told him. "I took over and did a good job for you, while you couldn't. You did the hard part, taking care of him after the shark bite, and again during his last few weeks. When he needed you most, you were there for him."

He sniffed and wiped his nose. "He changed a lot while me and Mom were gone."

"It was the cancer," I said, remembering how quickly Finn had gone downhill after the diagnosis. "He got weak really fast after you guys came home."

"And there wasn't anything—"

"No, son," I replied. "If there was, you know I would have done it. But as strong as he was, he was very old and weakened by the shark bite. Another surgery might have killed him, and even if it was successful, we'd probably be facing it again in just a few months. The cancer had spread too much."

"Yeah, but..." His voice trailed off.

"Look at it from his point of view, son. Being wheeled away by strangers in an unknown place, scared and alone, then never waking up from the surgery, or having the doctor come here and help him fall asleep on his favorite bed, surrounded by everyone he loved. Which would you choose?"

Alberto stared at the framed snapshot in my hands for a moment. "He was sure a good dog."

"Yeah, he sure was," I agreed. "He was my *third* good dog."

"You told me about Pescador," he said. "When did you have another one?"

"When I was about your age," I said. "Molly was a black Lab that Pap brought home when I was ten. She died not long after I was transferred to Parris Island for Drill Instructor School." I remember the pain I'd felt then. "I was a drill instructor and couldn't be there for her."

"How old was she?"

"A little over thirteen."

"How long did Pescador live?"

"After I returned him to the woman he belonged to, he lived to be fourteen."

"Three good dogs..." he said, his voice trailing off.

"Supposed to be four," I said, grinning at him. "At least, according to Scott Kirby."

He laughed and we both started singing Scott's song, *Four Good Dogs*.

"Mom said I have to wait until tomorrow to change the oil in the Maverick," I said. "We're going to the dinner concert at four."

"That's still five hours."

"Minus an hour to get ready," I said, kicking my feet slowly in the water. "And another hour to get there. By myself, it'd probably take... oh, maybe three hours. Not a lot of wiggle room."

"How about if I helped?"

I nodded thoughtfully. "Yeah, I think with your help, we can probably get it done in just *two* hours."

"Let's do it," he said, scrambling to his feet.

I got up and trotted after him as he sprinted up the steps. Savannah was just coming out the door.

"Me and Dad are gonna change the oil in the Maverick," he said.

"We'll get it done before we have to leave."

He dashed past her into the house, and I handed the photograph to Savannah.

"He's just missing Finn," I said.

She took it and looked down at it for a moment. "I miss both of them," she said. "Finn and Woden. Such an unlikely pair."

"Kinda like us?"

She looked up at me for a moment, the sun highlighting her hair and face in a way that would make a rose blush with envy.

"Go change your oil, swab," she said, pushing me in toward the ladderwell to the dock area.

I grinned and snapped a salute. "Aye aye, Admiral!"

CHAPTER THREE

With Alberto's help, I finished changing the oil in the big 300-horse outboard in less than two hours. As we were putting the cowling back on, he stopped me.

"Why's it say three hundred there," he asked, pointing to the air cleaner cover, "and two-fifty on the cover?"

"Other fishermen can't see what's really on the inside," I replied, lowering the cowl into place. "You don't always have to let others know what you have."

"I don't get it."

"Take *Gaspar's Revenge*, for instance," I began. "I never run her at what she's capable of when others are around. It's kind of a secret. Other people just don't need to know."

He thought about it a moment as I reached over and latched the cover in place.

"So... like if you're in a fishing tournament," he said, rubbing his chin, "and you had to go somewhere way across the bay, you wouldn't want the other guys knowing you can beat them?"

"Exactly," I replied. "Or like with your karate lessons. You don't go around showing off—that's not what it's for. You keep that knowledge to yourself and only reveal it when you need it." I gave the cowling a quick wipe with a clean rag, then stood up. "We better go get cleaned up."

I followed Alberto up the steps and spotted Savannah through the window.

"Mom's out in the garden with Naomi," I told Alberto. "Why don't you get in the shower first, and I'll go give them a hand."

He disappeared into the head, and I went out to the back steps, then down to the garden.

"He was horrible," Naomi was saying.

"Who?" I asked. "Jimmy?"

"This jerk in the parking lot at Publix yesterday," Naomi said. "A girl sort of gets used to it when she's alone. But when you're with your boyfriend?"

"What'd he do?" I pressed.

"Made a vulgar gesture with his crotch," Naomi replied. "Right in front of Jimmy, too."

"What'd Jimmy do?" I asked but could guess the answer.

Jimmy Saunders had been my first mate and only employee almost since I arrived in the Keys. He was a peaceful man, preferring to live his own life on his own terms and not be bothered.

"I think he did it more to taunt Jimmy than anything," she said. "He was an ugly little man—much smaller than Jimmy. But when Jimmy started toward him, the guy dropped the tailgate on his pickup and there were two big, mean-looking dogs ready to pounce. The guy laughed and got in his truck, then took off so fast the dogs almost fell out."

"Pit bulls?" I asked.

There was an overabundance of the breed in South Florida. Many times, the owners were gangsters or drug dealers, and used the big dogs as status symbols, often pitting one against another in a fight to the death.

"No," she replied. "One looked like Woden and the other like Finn, but black."

"A Rottweiler and a black Lab?"

"I think so," Naomi replied.

Savannah touched my arm, and I felt the tension ease a little. People who bullied others for fun just rubbed me the wrong way. But those who were cruel to an animal that wanted no part of their barbaric games needed to have their penis clamped in a locked vise while the shed was on fire and given only a dull, rusty butter knife.

I never bought into the "mean breed" thing. As I'd explained to Alberto not three hours earlier, dogs are born to love unconditionally. But if the only human contact they get is a backhand or a kick, they quickly learn to hate and fear.

People who were mean to animals ranked at the top of my bully list.

"He'll get what's coming to him one day," I said with a sigh. "Karma always comes back around to bite mean people in the ass."

"Where's Alberto?" Naomi asked Savannah. "He's usually like your little shadow."

"He's getting a shower," I replied. "We're going to the community theater in a couple of hours."

"Jimmy and I went last week," Naomi gushed. "It was *very* nice, kind of romantic."

"He won't be long," I told Savannah. "If you want to get in there next, I think I'll go for a swim."

"Be careful," she said, touching my arm again. "It's been a while."

I left them and walked back to the house. I used to swim three times a week and wanted to get back into that routine, so I opened a small outdoor storage bin and grabbed my swimming goggles and a small, drawstring bag. Then I went out onto the pier, slinging the bag over my head and left shoulder.

The water in my dredged channel and turning basin, as well as in the dock area below the house, was six to seven feet deep, with the dredging spoils on either side rising almost to the surface. Shallow, three-foot banks extended beyond them, all the way out to Harbor Channel, and wrapped completely around the island.

My channel ran southeast to the nearest part of Harbor Channel, about two hundred feet from the end of the pier. There, the bottom dropped quickly to thirty feet in places along the three-mile natural channel. It ran northeast to southwest before dissipating into the backcountry.

At the other end, where it flowed into the Gulf of Mexico, was where Mac Travis and Mel Woodson lived. Their island was almost two miles away and was once my turnaround.

At the end of the pier, I stretched for a few minutes, then pulled the goggles over my eyes and dove in. When I reached the spoils on the other side, I found the gap I'd created for my kayak and easily swam through.

Continuing slowly across the bottom, I angled toward the main channel for a moment, startling a small green turtle foraging in the turtle grass.

Once I came to the surface, I took a breath and struck out eastward in a slow crawl, inhaling every other right stroke, and slowly exhaling between.

It was a technique a friend had taught me a long time ago that slows the heart rate and allows a free diver to be calmer, which extends the length of time they can stay underwater. Simply by inhaling normally, then exhaling slowly, the brain is triggered to release a chemical called acetylcholine, which slows the heart rate.

A slower heartbeat means oxygen stays in the blood longer and more importantly, it slows the buildup of carbon dioxide.

I continued slowly across the flats, the bottom so close I touched it with my fingertips several times.

As my right hand passed the midpoint of its stroke, I turned my head, rolling my shoulders to inhale until my arm came over and forced my face back under. Then I slowly exhaled for three more strokes.

By the time I reached the edge of Harbor Channel, I felt more relaxed and focused. On my breathing stroke, I took only a half breath to give me neutral buoyancy, then dove over the edge, swimming slowly along the drop-off five feet below the surface.

I saw quite a few lobsters tucked back into crevices that sport divers couldn't catch. The twice daily influx and outflow of billions of gallons of water was what created the deep channel, scouring the sand away and leaving the limestone karst the Keys are made of.

Some of the cracks and fissures in the channel walls reached deep into the bedrock, twisting, falling, turning, rising, and angling through a labyrinth of rock.

A lobster could disappear into one of them and reappear twenty feet down the wall, or through some crack in the shallows thirty feet away.

During lobster season, divers came out to the edge of the Gulf because they were plentiful out here. The experienced ones anchored off Content Passage, but every now and then, someone would come around Upper Harbor Key and into Harbor Channel to try their luck.

They almost always came up after the first exploratory free dive all excited about how many lobsters they saw. Then they'd don their scuba gear and spend an hour on the bottom, only to come up with an empty goody bag and a feeling of dejection.

Before Finn got sick, he would swim with me most days, and we'd go all the way to Mac and Mel's place and back, almost four miles. He was the only other living being I knew who had that kind of endurance, aside from Charity Styles.

My youngest daughter, Florence, could beat me in a sprint, but after a mile, even she started to slow down.

I didn't mind swimming alone, but it had sure been more enjoyable when Finn came along. We often stopped at the turnaround if we saw Mac. And Mel always had a freshwater bowl and a dog biscuit.

Unlike a lot of dogs, Finn didn't have to expend energy to float. He was a Lab mix, and they have a dense undercoat that traps tiny air bubbles. But when they *did* become energetic, with their long legs and webbed skin between the toes of all four feet, they were just plain athletic in the water.

When I got to a small finger channel that reached up between my island and Mac's, I stopped and stood up, pulling my goggles down around my neck.

I was a little past the halfway point between our islands, standing in water that was barely above my waist. Yet, I was nearly a mile from any dry land.

There were a lot of places like this in the backcountry, where you could stand in shallow water and not even *see* land. It was an odd feeling for some people, being completely alone and isolated in the ocean and being able to stand on the bottom.

It gives a person some idea of what it would be like stranded alone in a vast ocean. Some are overcome by overwhelming emotion. For first- timers, even standing on the bottom, as I was, didn't shake the depth of that vast loneliness.

I felt it.

Finn had been a near constant companion for over a decade, right there with me through a lot of ups and downs. He'd risked himself to help me on more than one occasion and had saved Alberto's life.

I looked all around at the familiar positions of the many islands, the turquoise and yellow sandbars, and the deep blue of the channel, half expecting him to be slowly paddling around me, looking up expectantly, ready to get back in the race.

Suddenly, I felt very lonely.

Alberto was right. Dogs *should* live as long as people.

Lowering myself slowly back into the water, I paused in a squatting position, looking around at the acres of healthy turtle grass.

There were occasional small cracks in the underlying limestone, a few coquina ledges, and occasional coral formations. It was too shallow for most corals, and some areas were exposed on a low spring tide.

So, what dominated my vision were the slender, yellow-green blades of turtle grass. Shallow water can have lower oxygen levels, so the healthy turtle grass beds helped sustain a very diverse aquatic community.

A really big Nassau grouper swam slowly down the narrow cut toward the deep water of Harbor Channel. It disappeared over the edge to forage for his dinner.

The dinner concert.

It was Savannah's idea. A way of introducing Alberto to arts and culture. Dinnertime was about the only time he'd sit still long enough.

I pushed off the bottom and started my swim back toward the island, angling away from Harbor Channel on a different course

19

across the grass bed, since I hadn't found anything on my way out.

Just two minutes later, I came across the first beer can. I paused and picked it up, quickly twist-crushing it into a fourth of its size. Then I stuffed it into the drawstring bag over my shoulder.

I looked carefully around the whole area. It had been my experience that wherever I found one, I'd usually find more.

There were four cans in all. I crushed each one and put them in the bag, then continued my swim home.

Up until the past summer, the cleanup swim had been something I did every other day, but it had been a while.

I was a little surprised that the cans, plus a lure and monofilament leader I'd found halfway back, were all the trash I'd collected.

Of course, I'd only swum half of what I normally did.

It would be a pleasant thought to assume people were becoming better stewards of the sea. But if this past summer's annual sport divers or "mini" season, it didn't look that way.

A squabble over who "owned" an apparently good lobster hole had ended up in gunfire. The only injury was an innocent woman on a completely different boat over a hundred feet away.

From the deck of Jimmy's house, using binoculars, we'd counted more than thirty boats spread along the shallow reef north of Content Passage that day.

When I'd first built my little stilt house, more than twenty years ago, I rarely saw a boat anywhere near my island for days on end. Now it seemed to happen more than once a day.

I'd come here to escape the ghosts of the past and had wound up making this place my home, and put down permanent roots for the first time in my life.

The ghosts were taking on human form.

CHAPTER FOUR

When I reached the pier, Savannah was waiting. I climbed up and dropped the bag, accepting the towel she handed me.

"How was it?" she asked. "You didn't bring very much back."

"Didn't swim as far as I usually do," I replied, drying my face. "The seabed looks healthy and there were a lot of bugs in the wall. Saw a humungous Nassau."

She picked up the bag. "Beer cans."

"Probably tourists who don't know the lobster in the channel are more elusive," I replied. "Found a fairly new lure and leader I can add to my collection."

Savannah was already dressed—a navy sundress that hugged her well. I felt the need to hurry.

"How long do I have?" I asked, taking the bag back from her.

I popped the lid off a small barrel we keep by the end of the dock and dropped the beer cans in. Whenever it got full, we'd lug it to the Rusty Anchor on a grocery run and dump it into Rusty's big recycling dumpster.

"We don't have to leave for half an hour," she replied, as we started toward the foot of the dock. "I was thinking about that man Naomi was talking about."

"The one with the dogs?"

"Someone should jerk *his* chain," she said, as we stopped at the bottom of the steps.

"I'm sure someone will, sooner or later. Karma's a bitch, but she's very consistent."

"I'll take care of these," she said, taking the empty bag and lure, as well as my goggles and fins. "You go get cleaned up."

I went up the steps as she headed around the side to the storage closet beneath them.

"And wear shoes," she called out from below.

I trudged up the steps. *Shoes?*

We didn't go to many places that required footwear beyond flip-flops.

"Hey, dad," Alberto said, opening the door as I reached for the knob.

I looked down at his feet. "She told you, too, huh?"

"Mom said it's a nice place and we can't wear flip-flops there."

"There's no such place in the Keys," I said. "But let's do it for her, okay?"

"When are we going to see the new boat?"

Stepping past him, I went into the house, and he followed.

"I was planning to fly up there on Saturday," I replied. "The boatyard only works Monday through Thursday, so we can check things out without being in the way."

A couple of years back, I began toying with the idea of a completely autonomous, long-range, exploration trawler—one that could be brought right into the shallows and anchored near or even right on the beach, but still be solid and capable enough to cross oceans safely.

And I wanted to do it without using a drop of fuel. So, that meant sail or a solar-powered electric boat.

Early on, I'd decided it would be a tri-hulled build, no matter which, to distribute the weight of the boat across all three hulls. Recently, manufacturers of cruising vessels, both sail and power, were moving toward trimarans. They were vastly more stable and, since three hulls carried the weight, they were much faster.

I wanted light weight, for even greater speed, but I also needed maximum strength for safety. Taking all that into consideration, I knew it would be expensive. But I couldn't get it out of my head. Until I started putting it on paper. Or more precisely, on a computer.

The hull would be carbon-fiber composite, and the whole skeleton frame of the big, trawler-style house would be aluminum. It would almost span all three hulls, providing great rigidity. The structure of the house was carried nearly the full thirty-foot beam, leaving wide, covered side decks on the outer hulls, which were called amas, a Polynesian term for "outrigger" that is used for modern trimarans.

I'd put notes on paper, drawn up rough sketches and preliminary blueprints using the skills Pap had taught me as a kid, aided by Alberto's abilities on the computer. Then I submitted my idea to a marine architect in Stuart, a couple hundred miles up the east coast.

Construction had started last year, and I hadn't been up there since Savannah had returned in July.

"Are we flying in *Ocean Hopper*?" Alberto asked, following me into the bedroom.

"*Island Hopper*," I replied. "It's not far."

I grabbed a clean pair of skivvies from my drawer and went into the head. I showered quickly and returned to the bedroom to find Alberto still sitting on the edge of the bed.

"Mom picked these out," Alberto said, patting a pair of khaki pants, neatly folded, and lying on the bed beside him.

"*Long pants?*" I mock-whined. "*And* shoes?"

"Mom said."

"I hope she knows what a sacrifice we're making," I said as I tugged the trousers on and pulled my web belt through the loops.

Then I looked down at my feet and wiggled my toes. "What if someone sees us?" I asked, a tinge of fear in my voice.

"We'll pretend we're tourists."

I laughed and went to the closet. A T-shirt was always my preference but that'd look tacky with long pants. I pulled on a plain white tee and grabbed a stylish-looking dark-blue fisherman-style shirt, which Alberto had given me for Christmas, to go over top. It had little fish shapes on it, no more than half an inch long, but they were colored red, white, and blue, in the pattern of our flag.

When I stepped out of the bedroom, I found Savannah in her recliner. She rose and smiled as I sat in my chair on the right to put my Docksiders on.

She was wearing a blue sundress with thin straps, and she held a pair of high heels in her hand.

"You're kidding, right? Heels?"

"I don't get a chance very often," she replied.

I looked over at Alberto. "I remember a Savvy who scoffed at things like art and culture." I grinned and winked at him. "And *shoes*."

Savannah had been barefoot and wearing cutoffs when we'd first met. *And* she'd been pissed.

"That's not true and you know it," she said, with a twinkle of mirth in her eyes. "I was raised by a true Southern belle, kind sir."

"Who you rebelled against all through school," I countered, "preferring the deck of a shrimp trawler to the dance floor of the cotillion."

24

I stood and put my hands on her waist. "You look hot."

Savannah smiled. "And you clean up well, too," she said, glancing down at Alberto. "Both of you." Then she looked up at me and smiled again. "We're fifteen minutes ahead of schedule. You can have one beer at the Rusty Anchor."

"Then let's get this show on the road," Alberto said, using one of Savannah's phrases.

We both laughed as we followed him to the stairwell.

"What boat are we taking?" Alberto asked, scampering down the steps.

I glanced at Savannah. "We'll take *Cazador*," I replied. "Mom's hair will appreciate the enclosed helm."

Grabbing the key to the thirty-two-foot center console built by Winter Yachts up in North Carolina, I pressed the button on the fob and heard the metallic click as the catch on the big, spring-loaded doors released and the coils slowly began to unwind.

Each boat had the same waterproof key fob, which simply cut the low-voltage power to a pair of electromagnets, allowing the doors to open without power.

I handed the key to Savannah, and she stepped down into the boat then moved to the partially enclosed helm.

The inboard diesel cranked right up, and after she studied the gauges for a moment, she looked over to me and nodded.

"Cast off, son," I relayed to Alberto.

Savannah put her heels in the overhead storage and started rolling down and zipping the side curtains around the helm area.

Alberto and I loosed the lines from the dock cleats and coiled a few loops in each as we stepped aboard.

Savannah nudged the throttle forward, and there was a rush of turbulent water against the seawall at the stern. After a two-count, with the boat moving quickly forward, she shifted back to neutral.

Once clear of the doors, Savannah spun the wheel to the left and engaged the transmission again, kicking the stern around smartly before straightening the wheel as we moved into the channel.

"This really is a pig at maneuvering," she mumbled, steering the boat toward Harbor Channel. "Two engines are so much easier."

"She's a pig only at low speeds," I said. "But she more than makes up for her slow clumsiness with a comfortable ride at cruising speed."

The trip down to the Rusty Anchor in Marathon took twenty minutes and Savannah drove the whole way.

And I was content to let her.

"Shift to neutral and start your spin early," I told her as she idled into Rusty's canal. "She doesn't steer at all in reverse. Then it's a lot of cranking the wheel back and forth to crab the stern around."

Aiming at the stern of the barge, Savannah shifted to neutral and turned the wheel to port. Without propwash, the rudder sluggishly began to turn the boat. With it, the stern would over-respond. The prop tunnel design of the hull was great for shallow water with the prop housed in the tunnel and the rudder just aft of it. But it meant over-steering in forward and no steering going backward.

"Reverse only to slow her," I said. "Rudder angle won't even matter."

As the bow neared the midpoint of the barge, Alberto stood ready to loop the big bollard on its deck.

Savannah reversed for just a second, bringing the boat almost to a stop while keeping her eye on the bow.

"I got it," Alberto said, as I moved around the back of the helm to get the stern line.

"Reverse till Alberto's line tightens," I said, readying another dock line. "Then to port and forward to kick her around."

In seconds, we had *El Cazador* tied up to Rusty's barge at the end of the turning basin and we traded high fives for a slick job.

"That was the best we ever did," Alberto said, beaming.

I smiled at Savannah. "I think you're right, son."

Even with the beamy Winter added to the side of the barge, there was still plenty of room for even a large boat to turn around.

Alberto darted across the barge's foredeck and jumped to shore as Savannah and I crossed over the stern to the concrete seawall surrounding the small marina.

Once her feet were on dry land, Savannah stopped and held my arm while she slipped on her shoes.

When we both stood up, she brushed her hands over her belly to flatten the material of the dress, as she shook out her hair.

Alberto looked up at the two of us. "Wow, Mom! You're almost as tall as Dad!"

Glancing over at her, I could see he was right—we were almost at eye level.

Her shoes had a one-inch platform at the toe and four-inch heels, which made her appear to be over six feet tall.

I leaned in and kissed her cheek, whispering, "Have I ever mentioned how much I like to climb?"

The hairs on her neck stood up.

"Hey, look at that!" Alberto shouted, pointing beyond the restaurant and bar.

"That didn't take long," Savannah said, looking in the direction he was pointing.

Where there used to be a concrete slab for boaters to store trailered boats, there was now a metal building, three times the size of the original slab.

CHAPTER FIVE

The industrial-looking metal building didn't suit the land or the other structures on it. Rusty's house, the bar, and Rufus's shack out back, had all been built more than a hundred years earlier.

As we walked toward the restaurant and bar, I looked the new building over. It appeared solid and functional for its purpose, which was to store boats out of the weather.

Rusty had been talking about it for over a year and it looked like he'd finally laid out the money to have it built. Or more likely, he traded something for it.

"Probably premanufactured," I offered as we reached the door. "They deliver it on a truck, and it takes a crew maybe a day or two to assemble."

I held the door for them and we stepped inside.

Rusty had our drinks set up before we reached the bar. A white wine for Savannah, Red Stripe lager for me, and a root beer for Alberto.

"I swear, I believe this kid gets bigger every time y'all come down," Rusty said. He leaned and looked over the bar. "Ya got shoes on?"

"We're going to the dinner theater," Savannah said. "Why is that such a foreign concept for you men?"

Alberto leaned back with his hands under his arms, grunting like a chimp.

"Guilty as charged," Rusty conceded. "I know the water, I know the stars, the wind, the fish... But that high-brow stuff just don't hold my interest long."

Rusty's wife, Sidney, stepped out of the office. "Get used to the idea," Sid said. "You and I are going next week."

Rusty's head jerked around and his mouth fell open a little. "Huh?"

"It's a murder mystery production," Sid said. "You'll enjoy it."

"Murder mystery in paradise, huh?" my old friend grunted. "I guess that could be cool. I can always spot the bad guy a mile away."

"What are they doing tonight?" Sid asked.

Standing next to Rusty made Sid look even taller than her five-eleven. In bare feet, she was five inches taller than him.

And Sid's feet were rarely bare.

She'd once appeared in Playboy Magazine back at the time when Rusty and I were about to ship to Okinawa at the end of our second year in the Corps.

He'd hung her picture inside his wall locker and made me swear not to tell his girlfriend back home.

Rusty married his girlfriend, Juliet, shortly after we got back from Oki, and I'd been his best man. The following spring, with only a few weeks left of his enlistment, Juliet would go into labor early and die in childbirth.

Rusty remained a single dad until his daughter, Julie, was grown, rarely dating, or having any kind of social life outside his bar.

Then one day, a new beer delivery driver showed up at the Rusty Anchor—Sidney. Rusty had instantly recognized her red hair and long—but more filled out—figure.

He'd married the voluptuous redhead a year later.

"They're doing a full costume production of a scene from Shakespeare," Savannah replied. "Henry the Fifth."

I leaned toward Savannah and kept my voice low. "A dinner theater is one thing, babe, but Shakespeare? Don't you think that's a little heavy for an eleven-year-old?"

"Trust me," she said.

I looked into her eyes and saw that twinkle again. She was up to something.

"So, Rusty," Savannah said, turning away, "tell me about that giant building back there."

"That there's the new marina dry stack," Rusty said, as he polished a beer mug. "I can store thirty-six boats in there, up to twenty-eight feet overall length. And..." —he leaned toward me— "There's two garage doors and room for a full garage and four hotrods."

"Your Fairlane isn't in storage anymore?" I asked.

"For a coupla more weeks," he replied. "The garage side isn't finished yet. Wanted to get the storage functional first."

"So all the fishermen who store their boats *and* trailers here,,." Savannah began. "What will they do with the trailers? A lot of them stored their boats here because they didn't have room where they lived."

"She's right," I said, seeing a big forklift rolling up the new paved ramp that went from the building to the water. "The trailer has the same footprint, loaded or empty."

The forklift looked brand-new, with an enclosed, and probably air-conditioned, cab. Inside, the operator was barely visible through the smoked glass. He had blond hair past his shoulders and appeared on the smallish side.

"For them folks," Rusty explained, nodding in agreement, "the trailers can be left parked along the edge of the property. That actually ain't too many. Most stored here for the proximity. Now they won't even have to hitch up and back their boats in. They just call ahead, and my new "boat wrangler" will put their boat in the water and check it over."

I tore my eyes from the forklift for a second. "Boat wrangler?"

Outside, the big Taylor forklift came to a stop beside the building and the forks descended to the ground.

"Kid just arrived from up north," Rusty said. "Way up north—Wyoming."

"There's a move that'll cause some culture shock," I said. "A cowboy in the tropics."

"Not exactly," Sid said, as a pretty young blonde I'd never seen came in through the back door.

"Number fourteen is in the water, Uncle Rusty."

"Uncle?" I asked, looking from my friend to the young girl and back again.

"Well, more like distant cousins," Rusty said. "This is Madison Thurman, my third-great-grandpa's brother's fifth-great-granddaughter. Like a fifth cousin, twice removed, or somethin'."

Rusty could trace his lineage in the Keys all the way back to the early 1800s, and knew his family history in New England a hundred years before that, and back to Norway several hundred years before that even. Most of his ancestors had lived on or near the sea.

"That'd be Captain Thurman, who first settled here?" I asked, standing to meet the girl.

"Yup," Rusty replied. "Captain Augustus Thurman left Massachusetts in 1838. His kid brother, Cecile, had a son who headed west after the War of Northern Aggression and became a mountain

32

man, then a cattle rancher."

"Hello, Madison," Savannah said, smiling at the girl. "It's so nice to meet you. Rusty is like family. I'm Savannah, and this is my husband, Jesse, and our son, Alberto. Jesse and Rusty have been friends for over forty years."

We spent a few minutes getting to know Rusty's cousin. She was going to be living with them for a while, until she decided whether or not she was going to stay, and if she did, buy a house. She'd been a forklift operator at a bentonite plant in a little town called Greybull, west of the Big Horn Mountains, and when her mother passed away, leaving her a house and ten thousand acres, she'd decided to sell and go somewhere warmer.

"My agent already has two offers," Madison said, sounding positive. "And they include offers for the oil and mineral rights."

"There's oil?" Rusty asked.

"Five producing wells," she replied. "And one working gold mine that produces less than one troy ounce a week. But the wells only produce for nine months of the year. The oil's too thick to pump from December through February."

I could see the sparkle in Rusty's eyes at the mention of gold. He'd found his share of bright, shiny stuff over the years, but the lure of treasure still sparked his imagination.

"Brr," Savannah said with a shiver. "Cold isn't a problem here. We had a really cold spell this past winter, but it never got below fifty."

Madison laughed. "Low fifties is a typical summer night in the Northern Rockies and during the day, it's blazing hot and dry."

"What was it like when you left?" Sid asked, then turned to Savannah. "She flew out of Casper yesterday morning."

"High twenties," she replied. "But it was sunny. About normal this time of year."

"Sunny only matters if you can feel it on your skin," Rusty said.

"We don't get extreme heat here either," Savannah said. "There's always a sea breeze. But the humidity is high all year long."

"So what brings a Wyoming cowgirl to Gulf Stream waters?" I asked.

She glanced nervously at Rusty, and he nodded.

"I didn't have any family left there," she said, a bit meekly. "For several generations, my ancestors have been only children—no siblings, like me. When Mom passed, I didn't have anything holding me there except the land. No brothers, sisters, or cousins that I knew of. Dad had always talked about his family history going back to Nantucket, and the relatives we might have down another branch of the family tree. I found Uncle Rusty on Facebook, called the bar, and we talked family history until we hit on a common ancestor."

"My fourth great-grandpa," Rusty said. "Thadeus Thurman."

"Thadeus was a whaling ship captain in Nantucket," Madison said, obviously enjoying the history, much like Rusty, himself. "It was his grandson, Jeremiah Thurman, who went west in 1867, and became an honest-to-goodness mountain man, living off the land. He was educated too, and kept records of everywhere he traveled, finally settling in the Bighorn Basin, on the land I'm now selling."

Her smile faded and she looked over at Rusty again.

He nodded. "Jesse here is the friend I told you about."

"Well... there was a man I needed to get away from, too. He wanted—"

"*A Cowboy in the Jungle*," Alberto interrupted. "The Jimmy Buffet song."

"Oh, I loved his music," Madison said, smiling brightly. "He used to live here, right?"

"Down in Key Weird," Rusty said. "But he lived mostly in a palace up in Palm Beach and another on Long Island, where he passed."

"I wish there were more singers like him," she said, glancing out at the water beyond the backyard. "Listening to his songs always made me feel warm."

I laughed and looked at Rusty. "You didn't tell her?"

"Tell me what?" she asked, turning back to face us.

"Who's playing tonight, Sid?" Savannah asked.

The Rusty Anchor once had live music only on Friday and Saturday night, and often it was just a local fisherman who knew three chords and most of the words to a couple of Buffett songs.

But Sid had a contact list of musicians that rivaled Rusty's list of anglers, and now the Anchor had live music Wednesday through Sunday. And not just derelict guitar pickers whose boats broke down in Boot Key Harbor. Sid brought the top trop-rockers, as they called themselves, from all over South Florida, even a few beyond that.

"Scott is back in Key West," Sid replied. "He agreed to do one night here after he got settled in, and before he starts a regular gig on Friday at the Tuna. He should be here any time."

Savannah took the girl's hands. "If you like Jimmy Buffett, you'll like Scott. He's a blue-water sailor from a long line of Massachusetts sailing captains, and he tells stories in his songs, just like Jimmy did, and a lot of other trop-rockers."

"Trop-rock?" Madison asked.

"A whole genre of music has grown up around the parrot head lifestyle," Savannah said.

"And Saturday..." Sid continued, practically beaming, "Jesse Rice will play two sets, seven to ten."

"Really?" Rusty asked. "When did that happen?"

"I just got off the phone with his manager," Sid replied. "He was at Meeting of the Minds up in Gulf Shores, Alabama last week and played at the Flora-Bama, standing room only, so I was able to get him to come down for one night. But I had to promise him a day of fishing on Sunday, so I set him up with Dink."

"He's still fishing?" Savannah asked.

"Yeah, he'd prolly keep doin' it for free," Rusty said. "But the top anglers keep wavin' money under his nose."

Jimmy and I had found a small treasure hidden in the backcountry, at a spot where Dink had taken me cobia fishing. I was about to leave to track down a mass murderer I'd helped train, and had suggested to Jimmy that he bring Dink in as a partner, since it was his hole I'd fished and then dove the next day.

In total, they found 243 gemstones, mostly emeralds and rubies, and a jeweler in New York bought them all for a cool half a million, which Jimmy and Dink had split equally,

The owner of the boat Madison had just launched arrived, and she went with him, headed to the back door.

"Let's go check out the big forklift," Savannah said to Alberto, knowing that I would get to the part of Madison's story that Alberto had interrupted, and probably not need to hear.

Once they left, I turned to my friends. "Boat wrangler, huh?"

Rusty looked up from the mug he was absently polishing. "She welds, too, and has a good grasp of engines and stuff. And she ain't afraid of hard work—she's a Thurman."

"What did she mean about a man she needed to get away from?"

"That's the weird part," Rusty said, putting the mug down and leaning forward conspiratorially. "A total whack-job, bro. Keeps tellin' her she has to get knocked up this winter. Creepy."

"Former boyfriend?" I asked.

"That's just it," he replied. "He's just a guy from the plant she worked at."

I was sure there was more to the relationship than just being coworkers.

"Her property will bring millions," Sid added. "That's probably what he's after. But the timing's the oddest thing."

"Timing?"

"Jeremiah Thurman settled on Madison's land in 1870," Rusty said, putting the mug down. "And his firstborn was a son in 1874. Since then, every firstborn has been born in that same house, every single one a boy, and always within a few weeks of the father's twenty-fifth birthday in November. Madison turns twenty-four in a coupla weeks."

"You mean like, 1874, 1899, 1924—"

"Up to the year 1999," Rusty interrupted, "when Madison was born. She's the only firstborn child who was a girl in six generations."

"And this man back home," Sid said, shuddering like she'd gotten a chill, "thinks it's his mission to impregnate the girl this February, out of wedlock, so the child will continue the Thurman name on that land."

"And no doubt give him some tie to the land, too," I said. "The land she's selling."

Savannah and Alberto returned, and we got caught up on local gossip with Rusty for a few minutes—who was seeing who, who broke up, which guides were catching fish, and which ones weren't.

Rusty also told me about a theft, several weeks earlier, up on the mainland. Two dogs from Miami-Dade PD's K-9 unit had been stolen. I couldn't help but wonder if the pervert Naomi had seen was the thief.

He also told us about the annual fall influx of newcomers seeking shelter from a cold northern winter and a new life in paradise.

Living in the only tropical paradise in the country you could drive any rattle trap to, wasn't all it was cracked up to be. It was expensive, and if a person lacked a particular skill that was in demand locally, few lasted more than a season.

Madison had the advantage of having well-established family already living in the area. She was a forklift operator back home, and her welding ability and mechanical knowledge would be useful here. She also had apparent wealth and an outdoorsy attitude.

How much she would get for her property in Wyoming, I didn't know, but prices in the Keys for a small home on an eighth of an acre lot would probably be comparable to a six-bedroom farmhouse and a few hundred acres in Wyoming. But she would have a place to live, and likely a big pile of cash left over.

Time would tell if she could make it through the long haul. But she had a better chance than most.

We said our goodbyes and made the short drive to the dinner theater, where the meal was okay-ish. I could have done better using the rock in the fire pit and just an open driftwood fire and a few herbs. But the service was good.

As we were finishing dessert, the lights began to dim, and I could hear what sounded like horses' hooves moving nervously. But it was amplified and too loud. The volume was turned down and then came the clatter of metal on metal, except it didn't sound like it was coming through speakers.

I could hear tired whispers, coarse voices, and the grunting sound of a heavy man rising or moving. Someone coughed hoarsely, as though sick.

The lights dimmed further and a wide curtain at the end of the room was drawn back in the middle from both sides.

Stage lights came up revealing an incredible scene that caught my attention instantly. There were dozens of actors, all wearing heavy-looking suits of armor and chainmail.

Alberto sat up straighter in his seat, peering at the stage, where "fog" from a few liquid nitrogen pots on a parapet wall was rolling down across what looked like a meeting of the leaders of a regiment-sized encampment of medieval warriors.

This is Shakespeare?

My only exposure to Shakespeare's plays was acting out scenes in a classroom. The stage was phenomenal, and the garb and sound effects brought realism.

Large rocks, probably made from papier mâché, were strewn across the front of the stage. A catapult of some kind was off to one side and a ladder to the top of the wall stood at the other.

From behind us, barely audible at first, rose the sound of a chaotic battle.

CHAPTER SIX

The actors on the stage all appeared weary, their faces gaunt and smudged with dirt. The colors of their tunics were stained with mud, or maybe it was supposed to be blood. Most stared across the audience, as if observing a battle that raged behind us.

"Where is the king?" a man on the wall asked, his defeated voice carrying a slight English accent, but sounding almost princely.

A second man looked over at him from the center of the wall, then a third, far to the left, spoke softly as he, too, stared into the distance over our heads. "The king himself is rode to view their battle."

Historical English accents, all of them.

The man in the center cut his attention to the second man, who spoke as if measuring his words. Then he descended the steps to the main stage.

Lights in the front came up as he joined two other men at the front of the stage—older men with full beards, going to gray. They, too, were staring off in the distance, faces grim.

"Of fighting men they have full threescore thousand," he reported to the first of the older men.

"What did he say?" Alberto whispered.

"Shh," I admonished quietly, not taking my eyes from the stage.

"Listen closer."

"There's five to one," the first of the older man said. "Besides, they all are *fresh*."

His voice was as deep as he was big, and he sported a thick black beard, graying at the chin.

The next man, much older than the others, statelier in appearance, with a beard that was almost all white, but trimmed short. He nodded.

"God's arm strike with us!" he declared with great conviction, then sighed. "Tis a fearful odds."

The man from the platform turned his head to follow the gaze of the older men, apparently looking out over a battlefield.

The sounds of chaos from behind us rose slightly.

The other actors on the stage around them spoke to one another in murmurs, wishing each other farewell before their last battle.

"Oh, but now we had here but one ten thousand of those men in England that do no work today!" the man from the wall wailed.

Then a younger man, dressed in brighter colors—red, green, and yellow—stepped onto the higher platform from the far right. The platform was built to look like a parapet wall.

He was without the heavy armor and mail of the others.

The men on the wall gave way in quiet reverence.

"What's he that wishes so?" the young man demanded, his voice one of British aristocracy. "My cousin Westmorland? No, my fair cousin. If we are marked to die, we are enow to do our country loss; and if to live... The fewer men, the greater share of honor!"

I sat enthralled, watching the scene play out. Alberto had taken to sitting on his knees to be higher as he watched everything intently.

I'd read the St. Crispin's Day speech in school but had never really understood the old-fashioned way of speaking.

As Henry V spoke, urging his compatriots further, I thought of Tank, wearing his dress blues and a holstered sidearm, standing on that wall in the desert and staring down at a mob of armed men. Like King Henry, he seemed invincible, and the mob reacted as if they *knew* he was.

I thought of Pap storming ashore on Iwo Jima, fighting for his life against a well-fortified enemy with vastly superior numbers. Just as the French had on that battlefield on St. Crispin's Day.

I saw my father and his battalion being overrun by a reinforced North Vietnamese division in the early days of the Tet Offensive.

I knew the perception of invincibility was an illusion.

Then I recalled the time me and Rusty had faced down a trio of slave traders intent on capturing Savannah, as well as the innocent wife and two daughters of a man who'd chosen the same anchorage as we had during Hurricane Wilma.

As King Henry recited the only lines I could remember from high school literature, my chest swelled and my eyes brimmed.

"We few, we happy few," he whispered softly, not having to overcome a single sound from the audience. "We band of brothers. For he today that sheds his blood with me shall *be* my brother; be he ne'er so vile, this day shall gentle his condition, and gentlemen in England, now abed, shall think themselves *accursed* they were not here, and hold their manhoods cheap whiles any speaks that fought with us upon Saint Crispin's day."

The scene continued, with an envoy from the French asking for surrender and Henry driving him away with a pledge that he and his host would fight to the last man.

When the curtain closed and the lights came up, I wiped my eyes and looked around. A few others in the audience seemed moved, and Alberto was still staring at the curtain.

"You okay there, little man?" I asked him.

He looked over at me, his face blank. "Is it over?"

"Yes," Savannah said, her voice soft. "What did you think?"

He turned his gaze toward her and blinked his dark brown eyes again as a tear ran down his cheek. "They were very brave. But why would they want to fight so hard? I want to know what happened to them."

"Though outnumbered five to one," I said, recalling a presentation of the battle in a class on early Renaissance warfare, while I was in the Corps, "King Henry the Fifth won a decisive victory on that day by utilizing the terrain to his advantage, so that the French were unable to send their full forces against him. In the confines of the open area between two dense forests, Henry's army fought against an even number of French, but when a French soldier fell, another took his place. The English didn't have to fight five times as many soldiers, they had to fight five times as hard. As for why?"

I thought for a moment before continuing. "War is barbaric, son. No matter when or how it is fought. King Henry crossed the English Channel, invaded a sovereign nation, and claimed the French throne due to some distant relative having gotten a French girl pregnant. But in his mind, and in the minds of his soldiers and countrymen, he was right, so they fought for honor."

"And you?" Savannah asked me. "Did you enjoy the play?"

I glanced at the stage. "It's a lot easier to understand when you see it acted out with such realism, rather than just reading it."

We left and started back to the Anchor, none of us talking very much until we were almost at the turnaround.

"Have you ever seen the Rocky Mountains?" Savannah asked, as I made the U-turn to get to Rusty's driveway.

"Flew over them a few times," I replied, turning onto the crushed shell drive and continuing slowly through Rusty's primordial jungle. "I went through mountain warfare training near Bridgeport, California, in the Southern Rockies. That's about four hundred miles north of the Marine base at Twenty-Nine Palms, and right on the Nevada border. Silver country."

"I'd like to see them one day," Savannah said.

"I'd love to see Yellowstone," I agreed. "Let's do it. Fly out there and spend a week or two."

"When?" Alberto asked excitedly from the back seat.

"Next summer," I replied. "Early, though. If it's as hot and dry as Madison said, I might turn into dust."

"I'd like to see it in winter," Savannah said softly. "It sounds beautiful."

I backed *The Beast* under its tree, and we got out, my eyes sweeping the area out of habit. *The Beast* was my 1973 International Travelall. It'd been modified everywhere but the body, which was light blue in most vertical places, with rust streaks here and there, and surface rust on most of the horizontal parts. It wouldn't get any worse, though. The body had been thoroughly cleaned and sealed with clearcoat. The engine was a Cummins diesel, and the interior was all modern.

As we started across the now half-full parking lot, a man's voice called out from behind us.

"Yeah, baby! Move that ass!"

Savannah and I both turned around. My eyes fell on a scrawny-looking man grabbing at his crotch and staring lewdly at my wife. His other hand was on the handle of a truck's tailgate.

The stolen police dogs.

At least I hoped.

"No, Jesse," Savannah said, as I started toward the man.

"*No, Jesse,*" the creepy-looking guy said in a mock falsetto. "Better listen, old man."

He dropped the tailgate and two dogs rose as one—a huge Lab, whose coat was darker than night, and a Rottweiler with a head the size of a bowling ball.

Both started barking furiously, but they were focusing on him as much as me.

I didn't slow or even break stride as I kept advancing. I raised my left hand, palm out, and angled slightly. "*Nein!*" I commanded the dogs. "*Platz!*"

Woden had been Savannah and Florence's defender for many years and was highly trained for protection duty. His trainer had used a mixture of English and German commands, the latter when the dog was "working" or on duty. *Nein* meant no, and *platz* was the command for down.

The two stolen K-9s instantly stopped barking and dropped to their bellies on the floor of the truck bed. But they were still fully alert, giving me a curious, yet expectant look.

The vulgarity he displayed angered me to the core, as I'm sure it had Jimmy. But my first mate was, at best, neutral about confrontations and violence, and preferred to just be left alone.

I wasn't Jimmy.

I know I'm an old man. And the gray hairs and lines in my face identify me as such to others. But I really don't like it being thrown in my face as if I'm some decrepit has-been.

And what I really hated was men who bullied or harassed women.

I stopped four feet away, ignoring the dogs.

The cretin had a look of shock on his face as his eyes cut back and forth between me and the dogs.

"You wanna grab that pencil dick again, shit-for-brains?" I snarled, my voice low and menacing, body tensing for any weapon he might produce. "I'll show you what an *old* school ass-kickin' feels like."

Suddenly, Alberto was at my side, glaring up at the guy. "And I will fight with him."

I saw fear in the little man's eyes. At six-three and two-twenty, I was a head taller and at least seventy pounds heavier, with the weight still all in the right places.

And I was highly skilled at hurting people.

The guy turned and ran for the open door of his idling truck, where he jumped in and tore out of the parking lot, the poor dogs in back getting bounced around.

"I got his tag number," Savannah said, pulling her phone out. "I'm calling the police."

"What were you thinking?" I asked, crouching next to my son.

He turned to face me. "You took away his advantage. Just like King Henry did."

"So you decided to *turn* the advantage?" I asked. "Don't ever do that, son. I had everything under control."

His eyes darted back and forth from one of mine to the other. "I'd do *anything* for you and Mom. Just like King Henry's men."

"That's play-acting," I said. "The reality is that thousands of men lost their lives in that battle, and you might have been hurt in this one."

Savannah put her phone back in her small purse. "They're on the way. I gave them a description of the truck and the tag number." She knelt beside me, taking Alberto's hands in hers. "Are you okay?"

He shrugged and allowed her a side hug.

A few minutes later, a Monroe County Sheriff's cruiser pulled into the parking lot, and I waved him over. A young deputy I didn't recognize got out and approached us. His nametag read *Munson*.

"Are you the one who called about the kidnapped police dogs?" he asked me.

"Yes," I replied. "I'm Jesse McDermitt, and this is my wife, Savannah, and our son, Alberto."

"My name is Deputy Munson," he said. "With the Monroe County Sheriff's Office. Did you saw the dogs?"

"We all saw them," Savannah replied. "A black Lab, larger than usual, and a Rottweiler."

I nodded. "They were in the back of a man's pickup who's not from around here."

"How do you know he's not from the area, Mr. McDermitt?"

"Same way I know you aren't," I replied. "I've never seen either of you and I've lived and worked here almost twenty-five years."

He nodded, making a note on an electronic pad. "Why do you think they were the kidnapped dogs?"

"You mean stolen, right?" I asked. "Or did the guy make a ransom demand?"

"We're not talking about personal property," Munson replied seriously. "The two kidnapped dogs are working K-9 officers with Miami/Dade PD. If the dogs you saw *were* them, and the man you saw was who *took* them, he will be charged with two counts of kidnapping a police officer."

"Charge him with being a turd-fondling pervert, too," I mumbled.

"Excuse me?"

"I know they were the right dogs. They both obeyed German commands."

"What did he command the dogs to do?"

"He didn't," Alberto cut in. "Dad did. And the dogs obeyed."

Deputy Munson glanced down at Alberto for a second before addressing me again. "*You* ordered them?"

"We used to have a Rottweiler," Savannah explained. "Woden was protection-trained and when he was working, we used German commands."

He made another note and looked up at me. "That was a gutsy thing to do, sir. What if they weren't trained K-9s?"

I grinned and looked down at Alberto. "There are no bad dogs."

"Just bad people who treat them wrong," he added with great conviction.

I looked back at the deputy and shrugged. "I guess I would've had to rely on the fact that dogs just like me. Besides, you don't see those two breeds running together down here very often."

"Did the man say anything or make any sort of... gesture?"

"Come with me, Alberto," Savannah said, putting a hand on the boy's shoulder and guiding him toward the door of the bar.

I waited until they were out of earshot before replying in a low voice, "He made vulgar comments to my wife and grabbed his crotch, and it's not the first time. A friend had a similar encounter with the same man *and* dogs."

"Anything else?"

"He called me an old man."

Munson arched an eyebrow.

"Okay, so that part isn't a crime," I said with a shrug.

"And what did you do?"

"I told him to grab his pencil-dick again and I'd show him what an ass-whipping from an old man felt like."

Munson looked up from his tablet. "You threatened him?"

"With extreme bodily harm, yes."

49

CHAPTER SEVEN

I knew what I was confessing to Deputy Munson. I knew what I'd done and said were against the laws of civilized society. But there are certain things I won't abide in my presence. And that creep had hit on two of the top three.

"You know I can arrest you for that," Munson said, staring into my eyes.

I shrugged again and crossed my arms, defiantly. "There's no complainant. And besides, one call to Sheriff Ramsey, and he'll pick me up and give me a ride back here."

"You know the sheriff?"

"Decent offshore angler," I replied. "But he's an artist with a fly rod in his hands. I'm a charter captain, retired Marine, and former DHS agent."

He stared into my eyes for a moment, then looked over to where Savannah and Alberto waited near the door.

"I don't know if your friend reported her encounter with this man," he said. "Short, unkempt, and looks like he was beaten with an ugly stick?"

I nodded.

"Including this one, there have been five such incidents reported in the last three days. But now we have a vehicle description and license plate number. We'll find and arrest this man. And when we do, will you and Ms. McDermitt be willing to testify?"

I knew the dance. It wasn't just a Keys problem. Cops in every city and town were overworked, understaffed, and grossly underpaid. It'd only gotten worse over the last few years due to the pandemic and the government's inability to handle it.

The problem was pervasive in every facet of society—boarded-up restaurants, shuttered movie theaters, skyrocketing home prices due to less inventory being built, slow service everywhere due to understaffing, first responders pulling double duty... The list went on and on.

Unforeseen consequences, the talking heads in D.C. cited.

Maybe to a thick-headed mule.

Unfortunately, if nobody was willing to testify or press charges, it didn't make much sense for the police to put a lot of time into making an arrest.

Except they were police dogs.

"Deputy Munson," I began, "we recently lost the second of two great dogs we'd had for a very long time. If it means getting those dogs out of that turd-fondler's hands and back on the job, you can bet your last nickel we'll testify."

He cocked his head, a look of amusement in his eyes. "Did you say *turd*-fondler?"

"Not politically correct, but I think it's appropriate for this kind of degenerate."

He gave me his card and asked me if we remembered anything else to give him a call.

Just as I reached Savannah and Alberto, the door opened, and Rusty stepped out. "What's goin' on?"

He was looking past us at the county cruiser leaving the parking lot.

"We saw the guy who stole the police dogs up in Miami," I replied.

"Kidnapped," Alberto corrected me, moving toward the door.

Rusty held it open for him. "Did he... uh—"

"Make a vulgar comment?" Savannah asked, after Alberto squeezed past Rusty and went inside. "Nothing most women haven't had to endure a thousand times by my age."

Rusty followed us inside and hurried behind the bar. "And he's still livin'?"

We sat at the bar and Savannah had another glass of wine. Rusty poured a heavy porcelain mug of steaming coffee for me, and a hot chocolate for Alberto.

"Even if it's ninety degrees outside," he said to the boy, with a wink, "on the first of November, it's tradition to drink hot chocolate."

"Whose tradition?" Alberto asked.

"Well, family tradition, I reckon—us Thurmans. There used to be a lot more of us here on this rock, though. So we're spreadin' the tradition to other semi-Conchs."

"Of course, Captain Augustus probably added a shot of homemade rum to his," I added, then gulped a third of the strong Costa Rican brew.

"I got his tag number," Savannah said. "The police will get him soon enough. And when they do, I hope he resists, and the dogs recognize the uniforms and help the cops."

"Karma always bites that kind in the ass." Rusty chuckled at his own joke. "Be good if she added some real *teeth* to it."

"Where's Madison?" Savannah asked.

"Up at the house. Been a long coupla days for the kid. Jesse fill ya in on the *hombre* back home?"

She shook her head and glanced at Alberto between us. He was looking up at the TV screen.

Rusty winked discreetly. He knew we tried to shield Alberto as much as we could, though we'd just failed miserably half an hour earlier.

I drained my coffee. "We need to get—"

The phone in my pocket trilled the call of a whip-poor-will.

I pulled it out and looked at the screen, confirming that it was my old friend, Billy Rainwater.

"It's Billy," I said to Savannah, then got up and moved toward the back door as I accepted the call.

"*Estonko*," I said, using the Calusa greeting.

"How are you, my old friend?" Billy asked, his tone serious.

I'd known William Rainwater, Jr., since we were little kids. His dad and mine had been close friends back in a time when it wasn't acceptable in some parts of the country for mixed-race social encounters. It wasn't nearly as bad in Southwest Florida as it was in places up north, though.

"Everything is as it should be," I replied, looking over at Savannah and Alberto.

"I'm happy she returned. You're a complete human being again." He paused a moment. "I have found something, Kemosabe."

"What?"

"Remember diving Truk Lagoon with your platoon sergeant?"

Billy wasn't usually paranoid about phone conversations, but I sensed that he wanted me to understand something without him saying it.

I glanced again at Savannah, my mind moving from civilian to tactical. She looked back, concern in her eyes.

I remembered that dive trip. Billy had just arrived on Okinawa, and Rusty and I were about to ship back to Lejeune. We all managed to get a four-day weekend and flew to Micronesia to dive the world's largest ship graveyard, with Rusty's and my platoon sergeant, Russ Livingston.

"Yeah, I remember that dive," I said, recalling a run-in the four of us had with a local black-market ring receiving stolen government property from U.S. Navy personnel.

"Remember the cigar that your platoon sergeant found that was big enough for all four of us?"

Cigar? He'd lost me. I'd assumed he was referencing the trouble we'd gotten into. None of the four of us smoked and I didn't remember anyone with a—

The submarine!

There were more than fifty sunken Japanese warships at the bottom of Truc Lagoon. And one of them was a small, four-man submarine. After the dive, my platoon sergeant, Russ Livingston, had said it looked like a giant cigar.

"Yes," I said, trying to comprehend where Billy might have seen a submarine. "I remember the cigar. Where did you find this one?"

"Way back, Kemosabe," he replied. "Two jerry cans of avgas back."

Aviation gasoline in the Everglades meant only one thing—an airboat. And ten *spare* gallons of fuel meant he was talking about somewhere so far out in the sticks, they had to pump in sunlight, as Rusty would say.

"How could it have gotten there?" I asked, very intrigued about a sub in the Glades.

"That is a very deep question," Billy said, and I could see his lop-sided grin in my mind.

I grinned back. "I'm a deep white man."

Billy chuckled. It was a running joke going back half a century between us, Matt Dillon, and Kitty Russell.

"I would like to get your help in exploring exactly how deep," Billy cryptically replied.

Even a minisub like the one we'd found toppled off the deck of a Japanese transport ship would probably need at least six feet of water when it was on the surface.

"Is it as big as the one we, uh... smoked?"

"Much larger," he replied without elaborating. "And I have a theory about how. Can you come here?"

"To LaBelle?"

"Yes," he replied. "I dropped a pin before heading back to cell range."

I glanced over at my family again. Rusty gave me a questioning look.

"I was planning to fly up to Stuart on Friday," I said.

"Needs to be sooner," he replied. "And Rusty has to come."

Rusty?

"I'll ask him, and if he agrees, we can come up tomorrow, then I can fly on to Stuart from there the next day."

"Text me when you're thirty minutes from the airfield. You'll stay at my house. How big a truck do I need?"

Billy owned a custom 4x4 shop outside LaBelle, not far from where we both grew up. Well, technically, his father still owned it, last I'd heard.

I glanced toward the bar again. "Better make it a four-door SUV."

"It will be good to see you both again."

For the past couple of years, Billy had been very involved in the affairs of indigenous people all over the world. Billy's father had been chieftain of the Calusa, but he'd been in a home ever since an accident took his wife, Billy's mother, many years ago. He was very old now and hadn't said a word in decades. William, Sr., or Leaping Panther, as his people called him, was full-blooded Calusa, one of only a few remaining.

Billy's mother had been half Seminole and half Calusa. Leaping Panther's peers, the other full-blooded Calusa elders, were all white-haired old men now, comprising the council, and Billy had taken over as chieftain, by virtue of being the son of the former leader and having more Calusa blood than any of the elders' descendants.

He'd felt bad that he'd been in South America when Flo got married and was unable to get out of the conference to attend, even if he'd known. He'd been working deep in the Amazon rainforest, out of touch with civilization for nearly a year.

"See you in the morning," I said, then ended the call and returned to the bar.

"What did Billy want?" Savannah asked.

I glanced at Rusty, then back at Savannah. "I think he found a submarine."

"Billy?" Rusty asked. "Found a sub?"

I looked over at him. "In the Everglades. And I think there's treasure aboard."

"Treasure?" Savannah asked. "What kind of treasure?"

"No idea," I replied. "But he wants me and Rusty to go with him to look at it again, and, well... Rusty's a licensed salvor."

"I'm in," Rusty said. "We ain't had a good adventure in a helluva long time."

"A submarine can't be in the Everglades," Alberto said, taking his eyes off the weather forecast and looking up at me. "The water isn't deep enough."

"Speaking of shallow water," Savannah said. "The tide will be too low in an hour to get across the flats, and we'll have to loop up around it toward Mac and Mel's house."

We said our goodbyes and headed down to the dock. In minutes, Savannah had the engine idling and Alberto was standing in the cockpit, holding the stern line still looped around a deck cleat. I pushed the bow out as hard as I could, then went to the stern and gave it a shove with my foot before stepping aboard as Alberto pulled the line in.

Savannah waited as *El Cazador* drifted at an angle, slowly moving away from the barge. Piloting the inboard center console took patience.

When the stern was far enough away, she turned the wheel and pushed the engine control forward until it engaged the transmission. The stern kicked around from the sudden rush of water against the rudder, and she straightened the wheel.

"Want me to drive?" I asked.

"Well, the helm's in the center," she said, leaning back against the post. "And I don't want the wind to mess up my hair."

I nodded and grinned.

She didn't care about her hair. She just wanted to pilot the boat and that was fine by me—I was happy to just let her. And to be honest, she was a much more patient skipper. I guess it came from all those years in her slow trawler, *Sea Biscuit.*

Thirty minutes later, we turned into the channel to the house, and I told her to just pull up to the pier. "We can bring her inside in the morning."

Jimmy and Naomi met us at the pier and helped tie *Cazador* up for the night.

"So, how was it, *compadre?*" Jimmy asked as we stepped over.

"It was awesome!" Alberto exclaimed. "I want to go see it again."

"Well, right now," Savannah said, "it's time for you to get ready for bed. I'll go up with you." Then she turned to me. "I'll be down in a few minutes, and you can tell us what you found out."

Alberto was halfway up when he stopped and called back, "C'mon, Mom."

"That sounded cryptic," Jimmy said in a low voice, as we walked around the side of my stilt house.

I could see they already had a fire going in the fire ring and we headed toward it. The old metal ring had been on the island when I'd bought it and it'd seen a lot of use. Driftwood was easy to come by, and the warmth of the flames attracted any mosquitos. So we tended to burn a fire almost every night. The ring had even survived Hurricane Irma, which had passed directly over the island, destroying almost everything else. It had taken a lot of work to make the island habitable again.

"Not really cryptic," I said, as we crossed the large clearing toward the fire. "It's about a distant relative of Rusty's. But let's wait till Savvy comes down so I don't have to go through it twice."

We reached the fire pit on the east side of the island, and I gave Jimmy the other news. "Billy called me about an hour ago."

"Billy Rainwater?" Jimmy asked, tossing more driftwood on the fire. "He still down in Brazil, man?"

"No, he's back," I replied. "And from what I gather, he's found a submarine."

"A sub?" Jimmy asked dubiously. "How deep? That coast has been mapped and remapped, and every structure that would attract fish has been marked. Lots of crab and lobster fishermen all the way up to Sanibel."

"He says he found it in the Glades."

Jimmy had started to toss a gnarled piece of what looked like sun-bleached mangrove onto the fire and froze, staring at me. "Was it German?"

"German?" Savannah asked, approaching the fire. "What in the world would make you think that?"

"It'll keep, *mi amiga*," Jimmy said, tossing the stick into the fire ring. "First, what's this about Rusty's relative?"

"Have you met her?" Savannah asked, sitting down next to me. "I liked her right off." She elbowed me. "And I think Jesse was impressed with her forklift skills."

Jimmy shook his head. "Forklift?"

"Rusty had the dry stack built that he's been talking about," I explained. "And as it turns out, this long-lost relative of his, who used to be a forklift operator, just shows up."

"Aunt Sidney mentioned that someone might be coming to stay with them," Naomi added.

"A distant cousin," I began, then went on to tell them everything Madison had told us about her inheritance and the nutjob who wanted to take it.

"You don't think he'll come all the way down here?" Naomi asked.

"No clue," I replied. "The whole thing sounds almost like some sort of cult, all that twenty-five-year stuff."

"It is a little on the weird side—all of them being born in November," Jimmy agreed, which, coming from a man who believed he was a conquistador in a past life, was saying something. "The odds of the firstborn of that many generations being a boy isn't all that big a stretch," he continued, "but all being born twenty-five years apart and all in the same month?"

"The same month isn't all that strange," I said, thinking out loud. "Count back nine months from November." I grinned at Savannah. "I know what I like to do when it gets cold in February."

"Since when has the temperature made any difference?" she shot back, smiling.

"Any one of those things can easily be explained," Naomi said, in her light Cajun accent. "Firstborn, always a boy." She held up her index finger. "Always twenty-five years apart. And always in November." She paused holding up three fingers. "Any two of those things would be a big coincidence in just a few generations. But all three? And for that long? Why, it's just bizarre."

"And this cowboy, or ranch hand, or whatever?" Jimmy asked. "He wants to be the unmarried father of Rusty's cousin's son? And he's insisting the baby be born next year? Man, weird don't even begin to explain that."

"The way Sid told me," I began, "his plan was to get her pregnant this February—willingly or not."

Naomi shivered. "A rapist who schedules the attack with his victim ahead of time? Way weirder than the little perv with the dogs."

"Oh, I almost forgot!" Savannah said. "He pulled the same stunt on us tonight."

Jimmy's eyes cut to mine in the flickering firelight. "Should we be worried about the cops coming here, man?"

"Savvy got his tag number," I replied. "We called the cops and I'm sure the guy'll be picked up soon."

"Chalk *one* up for the good guys," Naomi said, making an imaginary stroke in the air with her finger.

"I don't think the cowboy ever considered that Madison might leave after her mom passed away," I offered, thinking aloud. "Her family's owned that land for over a hundred and fifty years."

We all sat staring into the colorful flames in silence for a moment, then Savannah turned to Jimmy, the firelight flickering off the side of her face. "Now, why do you think whatever Billy found was German?"

He grinned. "Ever hear of the 'ratlines?'"

She nodded. "That was toward the end of World War Two, right? Some high-ranking Nazis using organized routes to escape Europe and get to South America?"

"*Correctomundo*," Jimmy said, nodding and leaning forward. "Somebody paid attention in World History 101. Not all the Nazis followed the ratlines, though. There were a surprising number of U-boats still out there and many captains helped the leaders of the Third Reich escape the hangman."

"And they decided the Everglades was a good place to make a new start?" Naomi asked, echoing my thoughts.

"Not all of them made it, though," Jimmy continued. "Some were sunk by American or Allied forces, and it wasn't until long after the war that it was discovered that a few of those subs that'd disappeared were carrying a king's fortune in artwork, jewelry, silver, and gold. The wealth of the victims of the Holocaust, man."

CHAPTER EIGHT

We woke before dawn, having put together a plan over the driftwood fire. We were all going to fly up to LaBelle, where Billy would pick us up at the airport and take us to his boat ramp. From there, Naomi and Savannah would take Billy's truck and hit some of the boutique shops that had popped up in town.

Alberto needed new clothes again, though he complained that he hadn't yet worn any holes in the jeans he got for his birthday a little over four months earlier.

After coffee and fruit for breakfast, I heard the diesel on the Winter start up, and carried a large dry case down to the pier. Jimmy had a similar box already pushed back against the transom. We'd bought a couple of high-grade dry boxes and found that, for holding clothes and whatever we'd need through a weekend or a week, even though they were bulkier, they were far better than multiple bags that couldn't get wet.

"How far along's the boat, again?" he asked, as I stepped aboard and stowed my box with his.

"The outer hulls—the amas—have been attached," I replied. "And the upper deck bulkheads installed, but no roof yet."

"So, nothing inside is finished?"

"The port ama has two guest cabins and a head," I explained.

"The starboard one is just the master head and storage. Both were built separately and were nearly finished inside before joining them to the main hull."

Alberto came down the steps from the deck carrying a large blanket, which he placed on the front bench. "That's in case we get cold."

Jimmy and I looked at one another and grinned. It was late fall and there was a crispness to the morning air, but it wasn't anywhere near cold yet.

Savannah and Naomi joined us, both of them with their hair tied back. They went forward and sat on the bench in front of the console, pulling the blanket over their knees.

"Let's get her turned around," I said to Alberto.

We'd done this maneuver many times. It was easier to turn the boat around using lines from the pier before backing it into the dock area beneath the house. I could spin *Gaspar's Revenge* around in the small basin with no trouble, but she had two engines, which could be used in opposition to spin her around inside her own length.

Alberto untied the stern line and, while I held the bow rails, he pushed the stern out with all he had. The boat drifted lazily as I continued to apply pulling and pushing pressure on the bow rails to keep it spinning.

With the wheel turned all the way to port, Jimmy dropped it into gear for just a second as I held the bow in place at arm's length.

The stern continued around, and I pushed the bow away from the pier to a full stretch again.

"One more shot," I said.

Jimmy put it in gear again, and as I tried to hold the bow from running over me, the stern drifted farther around, and he took it out of gear.

Then I was able to work the starboard rails and pull *Cazador* back up to the dock facing the other way, so Alberto and I could get in.

Jimmy stepped to the port side, letting Alberto get in the middle, and said, "Take us out, little man."

Though he *was* growing, Alberto still couldn't see over the dash, but quickly climbed up on the leaning post and bent forward to take the wheel. He turned it until the rudder indicator zeroed, then reached over and pushed the engine controller forward, engaging the transmission.

"I forgot to check the tide," Alberto said, steering the boat down the middle of my channel.

Jimmy turned on the chart plotter. "It'll be high in less than an hour," he said, pointing to a trail of "breadcrumbs" on the plotter from a previous trip. "You can follow this line across the shallows."

Jimmy had previous trips stored in the chart plotter's memory for various tides, which made it a lot easier to navigate the backcountry.

After unzipping the curtain on my side, I started rolling it up as Jimmy did the same on his. Then together, we rolled up the front part.

Turning into Harbor Channel, Alberto slowly increased the boat's speed until it climbed over its bow wave and began to plane. Then he throttled back just a little to keep *Cazador* on top of the water while using less power.

"Are you okay, Mom?" he shouted over the wind.

Savannah and Naomi were huddled under the blanket, talking, but both turned and smiled back at Alberto.

"Why, I didn't know you were driving," Savannah said. "That

was so smooth, I figured it was... Jimmy."

She laughed and Alberto looked up at me and grinned. "Slow is smooth..."

I ruffled his hair, which was being buffeted in the wind. "And smooth is fast, son. Well done."

He looked at the water ahead as we neared Mac and Mel's island, then glanced down at the chart plotter, adjusting our course slightly.

Knowing shallow water was ahead always put a feeling of doubt in my mind, though I knew the water around our island very well.

As we passed Mac's island, Alberto turned slightly more to starboard, heading toward the flats. I looked over and saw Mac and his mate, Trufante, walking out onto his small pier.

We all waved as Alberto turned more, the rising sun passing directly ahead of us as he followed the crumb line on the chart plotter.

I pulled my shades down over my eyes. The engine hummed quietly beneath the console and the swish of the white water on either side of the boat was the only other sound.

There was something about being out on the water early in the morning that always put me at ease. With a solid boat under my feet, flying across the glassy surface of the shallows was akin to nirvana.

As big and ungainly as *El Cazador* was at the dock, she was at home in the shallows. Anchored, the thirty-foot boat only needed thirty-two inches of water to float, and with the prop in the tunnel drive, she could skim across water that was only knee-deep.

Twenty minutes later, we arrived at the Anchor, where Rusty waited on his barge to catch our lines.

"Hey, Jimmy," he said excitedly, tying off the stern line. "I started digging after I got your email last night. Kept me up most of the night."

"Digging for what?" Savannah asked, as I killed the engine and we all started climbing out.

"The reason a sub might end up in the Glades," he replied. "And there can only be *one* way that coulda happened."

"What's that?" I asked.

Rusty helped Jimmy with his case, and I hefted ours to my shoulder as we trudged up to the parking lot.

"Well, discounting intentional grounding," he replied, looking over his shoulder, "which would likely only get a sub about half a mile to shore at best up in that area, the only other thing would be unintentional grounding when the water's higher."

"Like a daytime spring tide under a new moon?" Alberto asked.

"It'd have to be a lot higher than that," Rusty replied, as he and Jimmy set their box next to Rusty's old seabag. He stood and turned to face us. "It'd have to be higher than it's been in a million years, since a time when Florida was an underwater sandbar and reef."

"That's not likely," Savannah said.

Rusty nodded. "I was thinkin' a fifteen-foot storm surge mighta done it."

I snapped my fingers. "A hurricane!"

"Not just any hurricane, bro," Rusty said, as I opened the back doors of The Beast. "My pop was born during the Great Hurricane of 1935 and when he was nine, the Lower Keys got hit by another big storm. They didn't name hurricanes back in those days and that one was just called the Cuba-Florida Hurricane of 1944."

I'd heard the storm mentioned. It had crossed western Cuba late in the hurricane season and killed several hundred people. Then it had skirted the Keys, passing over the Marquesas, then made landfall on Sanibel Island.

"It would've taken a lot of errors for a German U-boat to end up close enough to shore in that area to be driven inland on a storm surge."

"Definitely would," Rusty agreed, obviously excited. "That bank extends out for *miles* before the water's deep enough for a sub. But think back to that time. Radar had just been invented and most of Germany's old diesel subs didn't have it. The cloud bank from a big storm like that would cover the whole Western Caribbean Basin and most of Florida and the Gulf, and it sat in place down near the Caymans for a couple days. All told, the sun and moon was hidden for days. So no way any mariners not familiar with these waters could get a position by the stars. Maybe they headed east, thinking they were south of the Keys and got shoved inland on the surge."

"A comedy of errors," I agreed. "But if it was a sub headed to South America, what would they be doing in the Gulf in the first place?"

Rusty clapped his hands together and rubbed them as Sid approached. "Man, I sure do love a mystery."

"You just be careful," Sid warned. "Madison and I can cover things for a few days, but if you break a leg crawling around on some old boat, we'll have to *hire* someone to fill in."

"Not gonna happen," Rusty countered. "If I gotta, I'll get one of those battery-powered, elevating wheelchairs. But I'll be back behind the bar on Sunday."

We loaded the two cases into *The Beast*, along with Rusty's seabag, then climbed in—Alberto sitting between me and Savannah in front and Naomi sandwiched between Jimmy and Rusty in back.

Ten minutes later, Alberto and I went into my hangar while the others unloaded the truck. We hooked the battery-powered tow motor to the ends of the front crossmember between *Island Hopper's* floats, and then I went around the nose to unlock the big, rolling doors.

When I started to shove one door open, Rusty joined me, pushing the other side open.

"Okay, Alberto," I called. "Nice and slow. Watch that the tail clears *Ocean Hopper's* wingtip."

He guided the tow motor as it pulled my 1953 deHavilland Beaver out of the hangar, her red aluminum skin glistening in the bright morning sunlight.

Once he had her all the way out, we disconnected the tow motor and, while Rusty and Alberto put it back inside, I did a thorough walk-around inspection, then we closed and locked the hangar doors.

Jimmy had already climbed in and had the cockpit windows open to let the stale air out. We loaded the luggage in the small storage compartment in the back of the plane, and I headed to the cockpit and settled into the pilot's seat.

After I went through the prestart and everything looked good, I stuck my face out the window and yelled, "Clear prop!"

With the mag and fuel turned off, I engaged the starter and "walked the prop," turning the big radial engine over through two revolutions to get any oil out of the lower cylinders. Before the advent of the electric starter motor, someone on the ground literally walked the propellor around to turn the engine over by hand.

It's still recommended, but I'd just changed the oil the week before and had hand-walked it then, so I knew there'd be little or no oil in the cylinders.

Liquids can't be compressed like air in an engine's cylinders, so walking the prop two revolutions opens and closes both the intake and exhaust valves in each cylinder, allowing any oil that might have collected in the lower cylinders to drain into the exhaust manifold, and subsequently burn off when the engine starts.

When I turned on the mag and hit the starter again, the engine turned two full revolutions, coughed, turned over once more, then fired up, running at a rough idle and belching smoke from the burning oil and rich fuel mixture.

I adjusted the mixture until the engine smoothed out and was firing on all cylinders.

"You take the front!" Alberto insisted, his voice loud enough to beat out the engine sound.

I looked back, and he was pushing Savannah toward me.

"I thought you *liked* riding up front," Savannah protested.

I grinned. Ever since they'd returned, Alberto had been subtly arranging for me and Savannah to be together more.

Now he wasn't being so subtle.

She turned and saw my bemused expression and smiled. We'd both noticed Alberto's behavior and had talked about it, agreeing to just let him play matchmaker. We were both comfortable in our relationship again.

"Might as well join me," I called out over the engine.

She came forward and sat in the copilot's seat, pulling her headphones on. Adjusting the mic in front of her lips, she spoke into it over the intercom. "What do you need me to do?"

"Just starting the pre-takeoff," I said, handing her the laminated card.

"Roger that," she said, turning the card around. "Flight controls?"

I moved the wheel left and right, visually checking the ailerons on both sides. Then I stuck my face out the window as far as I could and could feel the tension in the controls and at least see the shadow of the horizontal stabilizer and rudder as I moved the yoke forward and back, while at the same time pushing alternately on the foot pedals.

"Free and clear," I replied.

We went through the rest of the checklist, and then I announced our intention on the unicom frequency to any other flyers in the area.

"Marathon, Beaver November one-three-eight-five, taxiing out from east ramp parking to active runway zero-seven Marathon."

We taxied to the far end of the runway, where I stopped short.

"Marathon Traffic," I announced on the unicom frequency, "November one-three-eight-five taking the active zero-seven for takeoff, left turn out, VFR to the north."

Hearing no response, I released the brakes, bumped the throttle up, and turned into the wind as Savannah looked back and smiled at Alberto. "Let's get this adventure on the road!" she said, raising my hand with hers and pumping both.

I advanced the throttle to full and felt the powerful radial engine pulling us down the runway.

In the little mirror over the windshield, I could see Alberto sitting back and crossing his arms, a satisfied look on his face.

CHAPTER NINE

Flying low over Grassy Key, I banked *Island Hopper* to the left, and the Gulf of Mexico opened up ahead of us with Florida Bay below the starboard wing.

The fuel tanks were full, adding more weight, but we didn't even need half the runway to get off the ground—a testament to the Beaver's long recognized standing as a top bush plane.

We climbed through clear, still air to the altitude Miami Center gave us and I pointed *Hopper* on a direct line to LaBelle Airport, just east of my hometown—Fort Myers.

Looking at my watch, I saw that it was 0810 and announced over the intercom, "We'll be wheels down in a little over an hour." I handed my phone to Savannah. "Text Billy and tell him we'll be out in front of the general aviation building at zero-nine-thirty."

She took my phone and started typing on the little keypad as I leveled off.

Savannah touched my arm with the phone. "He said he'd be there."

I took my phone and shoved it in my pocket, then looked over at her. "Wanna take the wheel?"

I could see in her eyes that she did, and she nodded.

"My aircraft," she said, taking the yoke on her side.

"Your aircraft," I replied, releasing the wheel and raising my hands.

The flight across to the mainland was uneventful and Savannah asked me to take the wheel once we were over land again. Well, wetland, anyway.

I looked down at the southern Everglades, the giant river of grass that the Keys owed their beautiful, clear water to.

Before the roads, dikes, and canals were built, fresh water in the lower third of Florida moved slowly south, unimpeded by anything man-made. The tall sawgrass and the ecosystem it created scrubbed the slow-moving water clean like a giant water filter.

The Glades covered more than four thousand square miles and, aside from the occasional stand of bald cypress and mangrove, it was virtually treeless.

There were thousands of places down there where I could land *Island Hopper* with no problem at all.

Bass boats and airboats have crisscrossed a lot of it, and one would think that by now kayakers and canoers had seen the rest.

How could a submarine possibly be down there for nearly eighty years and never be found?

When we were five minutes out of LaBelle, I switched to the unicom frequency and keyed the mic. "Beaver November one-three-eight-five on approach to LaBelle from the south, ten miles out."

There was no reply.

I didn't expect one at mid-morning on a Thursday. LaBelle was a very small airport.

I angled toward the west end, banking over the town as we slowed and descended. I keyed the mic again. "November one-three-eight-five on final approach to LaBelle from the west, two miles out."

I moved the landing gear lever and heard the hydraulic pump activate and start whining. A moment later, it stopped with a clunk.

"Four green lights," Savannah said. "Gear down and locked."

I added more flaps as we approached the end of the runway and reduced power until we were barely flying at sixty-five knots. A light breeze was coming from the southeast, just off the nose, judging by the windsock.

Island Hopper soared over the threshold and then settled softly on the runway, well down its length. I didn't even need brakes to make the first turnoff.

She didn't need a lot of room to *land* fully loaded either.

I'd been to LaBelle's airport a few times, so I taxied to a tiedown spot not far from the general aviation building, where I knew a fuel truck was parked inside the hangar.

A man came out as I was going through the shutdown procedure, and Savannah got up and went back to greet him.

Alberto came forward as I was shutting the bird down. "She did good, didn't she?"

I looked up and smiled. "She did very good. Have you been giving her pointers?"

He smiled, then turned around and followed the others aft as I unbuckled my harness and hung up my headset.

Outside, I helped unload while we waited for the man to return with the fuel truck, then the others carried our gear inside while I tied *Hopper* down.

When the man returned and started to unload his stepladder, I told him that only the belly tank needed fuel, as we'd only used what was in it on the flight up.

"Thanks, Captain," the man said, hanging the ladder back on its mount. "Makes my job a lot easier."

He was an older man I hadn't met on my previous trips to LaBelle. I stuck out my hand. "McDermitt. Jesse McDermitt."

"Nice to meet you," he replied, shaking it. "Jackson Duggard. Beautiful old bird."

I thanked him and handed him my Amex Black card. "Please store my card after running it, Jackson. And add a couple of days tiedown. We should be back tomorrow; Saturday, at the latest."

"No need for that," he said, pulling a device from his pocket. He swiped my card through it, typed something on the keypad, and handed my card back. "You're all set."

"Thanks, Jackson," I said, then hurried to catch the others.

They were just going out the front door as I entered, and I could see a massive black Ford Excursion with oversized tires parked outside.

The driver's door opened as I exited the building. Double running boards scissored down from a recess beneath the truck and were long enough to access the front and rear doors. Billy climbed out, his graying, black hair billowing in the light breeze as he jumped down from the bottom step.

"Welcome," he said, spreading his arms. "Thank you for coming."

"What in the heck is this thing?" Rusty asked, gazing up at the truck from his diminutive height.

Billy smiled. "Good to see you again, too, my brother." He turned slightly, lifting a hand toward the truck. "This is what you might call a 'redneck limousine' around here. I call it the Frankencursion."

The tires were unusual and enormous, mounted on brightly shined, five-spoke, aluminum wheels. The tires had aggressive-looking off-road treads, were waist-high, and had no manufacturer's name or size, or any markings at all on the sidewalls.

"Everything should fit back here," Billy said, and we followed him to the back.

He pushed a button on his key fob and the hatch rose, well beyond my reach. Billy opened the double barn doors below the hatch and the cases fit side-by-side. I lifted Rusty's seabag and shoved it up on top of them, nearly at the limit of my reach.

Billy went back around to the back door on the driver's side. "I relocated the door handles," he said, pulling a handle near the bottom of the door, which was at chest level.

With the touch of a button, the rear seat back folded down and then the whole seat flipped forward into the footwell, allowing access to the third row of seats.

"Three smallest in back," Billy said.

Alberto reached up and grabbed a handrail, then quickly climbed up the two running boards and into the truck. He could almost stand up inside. "Wow! This is really high!"

Jimmy helped Naomi up, and the three of them moved to the back as Rusty started to climb up.

"Ride up front with me," Billy said. "I want to talk to you."

I helped Savannah up, then climbed in after her.

When Billy started the engine, I could tell it was a diesel from the sound until I closed my door, which felt far heavier than I would have thought. Then the interior fell to near total silence.

Rusty found the control for his seat and raised it, looking around at the other cars in the lot. "You could just about make your own exit with this buggy. What would somethin' like this set me back?"

Billy looked over and gave a rare smile. "Over a million dollars," he replied. "It isn't complete yet, but I will be delivering this to a customer in Dubai next month."

The tires, I thought.

"The glass is bulletproof," Billy explained. "The whole body is armored, and the tires are run flats."

"A million-dollar SUV?" Rusty asked, looking at the gauges and switches on the dash. "Got an ejector seat?"

"Only on your side," Billy replied, reaching for a switch. He stopped and glanced over at Rusty. "Just kiddin'."

Then his tone changed. "Did you find out anything?"

"You ain't gonna like it," Rusty replied.

"I didn't expect I would," Billy said, letting out a heavy sigh. "If there is Nazi contraband aboard, anything of intrinsic value will be returned to those who owned it or their heirs or their people, correct?"

Billy was a lawyer, among other things. One of those *other* things used to be *arms dealer*, but I didn't think he did that anymore.

"Yep," Rusty said. "And anything that ain't returned would be fifty percent federal property if the find is within the National Park, or half to any private owner of the property."

"My only interest is the sub itself," Billy said.

"Probably rusted away to nothing," Jimmy offered from the back.

"I do not think so," Billy replied. "You will see what I mean, when we get out there."

Billy put the truck into gear and headed toward the exit. The highly modified Excursion was large enough inside that the seven of us had plenty of room, and when Billy turned onto the highway and accelerated, I could feel the G-forces pushing me back in my seat.

"What's under the hood?" Rusty asked.

"A turbocharged Cummins L9," Billy replied. "With an Allison ten-speed automatic and full-time all-wheel drive."

"And the weight?"

"Almost six tons," Billy replied.

"Must be a pig on gas," Rusty muttered. "Tell me about the location where you found this sub. I mean the history of that particular place."

Billy shrugged. "Nobody has been there for eighty years," he said. "If it is a World War Two submarine, at least we can assume that."

"Not the *exact* location," Rusty said. "I mean the area. Any historical significance related to that part of the Glades?"

"The Everglades was established as a National Park in 1947," Billy replied. "*After* the war. But the National Park Service first began acquiring land for the park as early as 1934. The area where I found the submarine was added in 1945."

"Who owned that part of the Glades before that?"

"The State of Florida," Billy replied. "It was open wetland."

I could see the thoughtful expression on Rusty's face as he mulled it over.

Finally, he turned in his seat and looked over at Billy. "I think an argument *could* be made that if it is a World War Two sub, and it somehow ran aground way out there before the state ceded the land to the federal government, that might mean the park doesn't have a claim."

"How so?" I asked, leaning forward.

"Two government bureaucracies?" Rusty rebutted. "I can almost *gar-own-tee* that the land grant from the state named every piece of real or developed property that was included."

"I've read the transfer papers," Billy said. "They're very long and yes, include physical descriptions and boundaries of any developed property within its borders. There was even a derelict boat named."

Rusty thought for a moment. "What if the land was claimed by some other party."

"Like the people who inhabited the area before the first European contact," I suggested. "That part of Florida has been claimed by many countries."

"I have a question," Savannah said.

We all turned to face her.

"Do you really think I'll be able to drive this thing around in a mall parking lot?"

Billy laughed as he turned off the highway onto a side road west of LaBelle. "No," he replied. "I have a regular car for you to take. This is all I have right now that seats seven."

The pavement gave way to dirt and then Billy turned in next to his house and parked under a tree beside a yellow Camaro convertible.

"You can take my car while we're gone, and my home is your home until we return. I've packed supplies to be gone until sunset."

"The ragtop?" Savannah asked, opening the door to get out.

"The tank is full, and I serviced it last week," he said, then turned to me. "We should go if we plan to return before dark. I want to try to get inside it."

"Your blowboat carry four people?" Rusty asked.

"Six," he replied. "I have extra gas and cutting torches under the second row of seats."

"You really want to see what's in this thing, don't you?" Rusty asked. "I got a question you might not've thought of."

"What?" Billy asked.

"What if there's human remains inside?"

80

CHAPTER TEN

After we'd put our gear in the house, and I'd removed my go-bag from the case, we said goodbye, and Alberto and the women were off.

When I heard Savannah scratch second gear once she got onto the pavement, I looked over at Billy and grinned.

"You know she hasn't owned a car in decades, right?"

He started the Excursion and looked back at me. "Should I be worried?"

"Oh, she can handle it," I assured him, just as the Camaro's throaty roar and the squealing of tires could be heard out on the highway. "But she sometimes drives like a teenager, so you might not have as much rubber left when she gets back."

When we reached the highway, we turned in the opposite direction Savannah had gone and ten minutes later, we turned off US-41 onto a well-maintained, raised roadbed of crushed limestone that ran straight out into the marsh. Half a mile down, we arrived at a fish camp, built on what was probably once a shell mound.

"Tribal place?" Rusty asked before climbing out.

"Privately owned," Billy replied. "But yes, the owner is Seminole."

The screen door opened, and a woman stepped out. She was

obviously Native-American, with long black hair cascading straight over her shoulders.

"This is the owner and my partner, Trish Osceola," Billy said. "Trish, these are the friends I told you about—Jesse, Rusty, and Jimmy."

She stepped forward and smiled, showing tiny lines at the corners of her eyes and mouth, the only giveaway that she was even close to our age.

"So you're the famous Night Crawler I've heard about all my life," Trish said, extending a hand to me. "Or would that be *infamous?*"

I shook hands with her and smiled back. "Nobody's called me that in a long time."

She shook hands with the others, then took Billy's arm. "Still, you're quite well-known among my people. I have known Billy nearly as long as you."

Osceola was the name of one of the greatest Seminole chiefs, and not an uncommon name among tribal Floridians. I'm sure if I'd met her before, I'd remember.

She turned to Billy, kissed him, and said, "Don't be out after dark. You know your eyes—"

"We'll only be gone a few hours," Billy interrupted. Then he turned back toward us. "Around back."

We followed him around the side of the building, which was covered by weathered, rough-hewn cypress planks, impervious to insects and rot. The building looked as old as the swamp itself, but it had a metal roof that looked fairly recent, and about fifty solar panels covering the entire south-facing side of the roof.

We walked out onto a small dock area that had open water for at least a hundred feet out from the shell-mound island. There were

82

three airboats tied up along the face dock. One was huge, easily thirty feet long and ten wide, with seating for a dozen people.

"Partner, huh?" Rusty asked Billy, beating me to the punch.

"Is that business partner?" I asked archly. "Did you buy into her fish camp?"

Billy stepped down into his boat and looked up at us. "Trish is my *life* partner," he replied. "Now, as we like to say out here in the swamp, get in, sit down, shut up, and try to hang on."

"I don't think they'll let you get off that easy," Jimmy said.

"Yeah," Rusty agreed. "You can't just say she's your 'life partner' and let it go at that," Rusty continued as he stepped aboard.

I quickly looked the boat over. It had a dark green aluminum hull and two rows of three seats in front with the helm seat behind and slightly higher than the second row.

Behind the helm seat was a six-cylinder aircraft engine with a variable-pitch, three-bladed prop that looked to be made of carbon fiber. Beneath the second row of seats were a pair of five-gallon gas cans and something else covered by a tarp. No doubt the cutting torch Billy had mentioned.

"Best seating for balance," Billy said, ignoring the sophomoric taunts. "Jesse and Rusty, outboard on the bottom row, Jimmy, you take the middle seat on the bottom or top row." Then he grinned. "The second row is called Widow Maker."

"Why do ya call it that, man? Yours is higher."

"The seats and frame are titanium," Billy said, with a grin. "Any branch low enough to hit the second row will stop the boat."

"Not funny, man," Jimmy said, looking up at the higher seat, then plopping down in the lower middle one.

Ten minutes later, I understood why Billy was a stickler for balance as he pushed the airboat up to what I guessed was over forty miles per hour; the hull was flying over the surface with barely any contact.

My perception of our speed might have been off a bit, though. It'd been a long time since I was last in a fast airboat, heading straight at a wall of sawgrass.

I could tell by the pitch of the engine that there was still a lot of throttle left, too.

"How fast will this thing go?" Rusty asked, his voice crackling over my headset.

"What is it with you and going fast?" Billy said, turning slightly to avoid denser sawgrass, which could mean shallower water.

"Just curious is all," Rusty replied. "Unless you wanna tell us about your new 'life partner.'"

"We're going forty-five now," Billy replied, still not rising to the bait. "With just me and minimal gas in the tank, I've reached seventy miles per hour."

"So, who is she?" Rusty asked. "How'd you meet?"

I glanced back in time to see Billy roll his eyes. "I have known Trish almost all her life. She is the granddaughter of one of the Seminole elders."

"That explains who she *is*," Rusty continued, needling, "but when did this 'life partner' thing happen?"

"When I was ten, Dad took me and Mom to a tribal convention, and I helped Mom in the kids' room, mostly playing games with the little ones. I taught Trish to take her first steps that weekend."

"How come I've never met her?" I asked, regretting it immediately. "Sorry. That was presumptuous."

"It is nothing," Billy said. "I know many people you have never met. The same in reverse is also true for you. We walk different paths, know different people."

"And sometimes those paths reconnect," I said, recalling something Billy's dad had once told us a long time ago.

"You remember?" Billy asked. "That was the summer that your path and mine diverged and yours and Rusty's connected. Then all three paths joined on the other side of the world."

"Yeah," I said, looking over at my friends. "I remember every word Leaping Panther ever said."

"Trish and I have been friends for a very long time," Billy said, maneuvering into a long, straight canal and accelerating. "Sometimes we were closer than others, as *our* paths drifted and came together over the years, as we attended conferences and council meetings. Her husband died of cancer two years ago and she went to the conference down in Brazil last year, representing her people."

"Yada, yada," Rusty said, looking back and making a hand-rolling gesture. "Get to the good stuff."

"When we returned from the conference, we started seeing each other socially," Billy replied. "That was four months ago, and now we are partners in everything—Osceola-Rainwater, Limited."

Billy continued southeast, into the heart of the Everglades, following dredged canals where necessary, and flying across sawgrass the rest of the time.

I knew that Billy was more than just familiar with the area; he probably knew it better than just about anyone, but I also knew the Glades changed constantly, even from one hour to the next, as the wind changed and bent the sawgrass in a different direction. He was heading toward a waypoint he'd dropped on a navigation app on his phone, so it was unlikely he was following any visual cues.

Or maybe he was.

Anyone from the area knew Billy's father had been the best

tracker and Gladesman around, and Billy had learned the old ways from him very well. I'd also learned a few things from Leaping Panther. Not just about tracking, hunting, and fishing, but about myself. He was the one who'd given me my Calusa name, the night I was born—Night Crawler.

After almost ninety minutes, the boat slowed to just barely staying on plane as Billy crept forward.

"It's close!" he said, his voice crackling over my headset. "Keep a look out. The only part visible is the mast, which I almost hit."

"That it?" Rusty asked, standing and pointing as he held onto the seatback.

"No," Billy said, angling away and looking at his phone, mounted to his seat. "That's a dead cypress."

As we angled away from it, I could see that what Rusty had pointed out had looked vertical and straight a moment ago but was now leaning and crooked from a different angle.

"There it is," Jimmy said, pointing ahead and to the left. "Eleven o'clock."

If I didn't know to look for something resembling an antenna mast, I wouldn't have seen it. But where Jimmy was pointing, there was a single anomaly in the bent grass, which seemed to ripple in the light breeze. As we got closer, I could tell that it was the broken remains of an antenna, mounted on something that only rose a foot or so above the water. It was long and thin, like a small boat, completely covered in a dense coating of swamp slime.

"A conning tower," I breathed softly, as Billy killed the engine.

I looked back to see him stand on his platform and shake out a lasso, which he easily looped around the stub of the antenna, then handed down to me.

"Pull gently from the bow," he said. "It might break off."

We all moved to the front and, with the other three moving and flattening out the sawgrass ahead, I was able to pull the airboat close enough so that Jimmy could reach what looked like the top of an old, rusted handrail.

Jimmy gave a tug on the bar. "Still feels solid enough, which is surprising." He squinted up at Billy. "I doubt this is eighty years old, man. This bar would be rusted to nothing."

Billy stepped over gingerly, moving heavy muck off the surface with his booted foot. He bent and gently tapped the surface with a wrench.

There was an instant ring of hollow metal.

"The Glades are very low," Billy said. "The great River of Grass is merely a stream today. But just fifty years ago, where I am standing now would have been the muck at the bottom of four or five feet of water."

To me, that statement was more alarming than finding a submarine this far inland—Nazi or otherwise. Billy knew the Everglades as well as anyone alive, and if he said the water was down five feet in our lifetime, I believed him. The drainage canals we'd traversed to get to that spot hurried the flow of water, which was not natural. The canals were manmade, built to drain the land for farming, and to control the flow or water in the Glades.

Rusty looked fore and aft of whatever it was Billy was standing on, and I followed his gaze, trying to imagine a two-hundred-foot sub lying just a few feet below us.

I unzipped my go-bag and pulled a telescoping baton from an inside pouch, extending it to its full thirty-six inches and locking it in place.

"Hold my belt," I said, as I positioned myself so I could hang over the side of the boat.

Rusty nodded, understanding instantly what I wanted to do. He gripped my belt and told Jimmy to grab my right knee.

I lowered my body sideways toward the dark brown water, leading with my makeshift probe. I had to jab it hard through layers of muck, until I was all the way in the water to my shoulder, with my arm fully stretched out and my hand and wrist in the muck.

"Hang on," I said. "When I say go, give me another foot and I'll stick my head under to feel deeper."

"Don't get it bit off by no gator," Rusty said, bracing himself. "Savvy'd kick my ass."

"Go!" I shouted, diving headfirst and thrusting the baton through the muck another few inches. I drove my whole arm into the bottom, rotting vegetation swirling around my face as I pushed the baton deeper.

There was a metallic ring.

I drew back and stabbed twice more. The ringing sound was even more distinct.

Rusty and Jimmy hauled me up and I stood in the airboat's bow, dripping water, my left arm covered with slime from my armpit down.

"There's a friggin' sub down there," I said, raising my arm in realization. "It was preserved by this."

"*Friggin'?*" Rusty chided. "Ain't no women-folk or kids around, bro. Ya don't have to watch your mouth."

"Yeah," Billy said, nodding from the conning tower. "You wanna get that shit *overboard*, Kemosabe? You're messing up my pretty boat."

"Oh, yeah," I said, moving to the gunwale to fling the slime off and rinse the thick, brownish-green sludge off my arm. "There is definitely something larger below."

"I have two questions," Rusty said, surveying the sawgrass, water, and the biological detritus of eight decades below it. "One: How much does a sub weigh? And B: Is there a helicopter big enough to lift it? Cuz that's the only way this ship is gonna reach open water *or* dry land, either of which has gotta be at least thirty miles away."

"Um, you used numeric and alphabetic bullet points there, Rusty," Billy said. "But to answer one question, we are about twelve miles from Pavillion Key."

I was familiar with the island. It was on the desolate coast of Southwest Florida, and a popular camping site for kayakers and canoers.

"And another three miles to water deep enough for a sub," I added, looking around and imagining a tidal force powerful enough to carry a submarine this far inland. "That had to be some tidal surge."

"The Glades were deeper eighty years ago," Billy said. "I looked up the specifications of German U-boats. Most had only a fifteen-to-twenty-foot draft."

"Why are you convinced it's German?" Rusty asked.

"Who else would have a missing submarine in the Everglades?" Billy countered. "Any that we lost are known about, and to my knowledge, no other country has had submarines patrolling the Gulf."

My eyes cut to the conning tower. "Except Russia."

"That's *steel*, bro," Rusty said, pointing to where Billy was standing. "Old school steel used when they didn't know about magnetic imaging. Russian subs have either low-magnetic steel or titanium hulls, and neither one of those rings like steel."

Jimmy turned to Rusty. "Did that Cuba-Florida Hurricane have a big surge?"

89

"As I remember it being told, it made landfall in western Cuba as a Cat Four," Rusty replied. "The only storm data, even then, was first-hand reports of the landfall. It passed across the Tortugas as a Cat Three and hit Sanibel Island as a Cat Two with a lot of flooding. If it slowed its forward speed as it neared shore, like they usually do, I'd imagine it might could..." He trailed off, scratching his chin, and looking toward the west. "I suppose it *is* possible. I mean, there ain't no other explanation. Billy's standin' on the damned proof."

"I was tapping on the *top* of the hull," I said, looking up at Billy, "at least eight feet under water. When a submarine is on the surface, where its minimum draft would be measured, there's at least a foot of hull above water, so what I was tapping on is probably eighteen feet or more above the keel."

Rusty looked up at Billy. "That'd be at least twenty-six feet down, and twenty-four of that's mud."

Rusty turned and looked back in the direction we'd come. "How deep are those canals?"

CHAPTER ELEVEN

B illy poured gas from the first can into his tank as I studied the shape of the conning tower again more closely. Then I readied the second can and glanced back at the torch set Billy had uncovered.

"You can't cut it open," I said, handing him the second gas can and taking the empty.

"Why not?"

"What you were standing on is the aft part of the superstructure, slightly above and behind the flybridge and deck hatch. It houses the periscope and ventilation fans."

"He's right," Jimmy added. "What I tied off to is the handrail. The deck hatch is probably four feet down."

"If it ain't already flooded," Rusty said, "it will be soon after you go cuttin' holes in it. If it's possible to get that thing out intact, it's gonna be months down the road; canals'd need to be dredged, equipment brought in."

"To answer your earlier question," I said to Rusty, "if this *is* a full-sized diesel sub, it would take a fleet of more than thirty of the biggest helicopters to lift it. And that would be if it wasn't stuck in mud with eighty years of muck covering the entire hull."

"So how do we get inside?" Billy asked. "And how do we get the sub out?"

"Gettin' inside's the easy part," Rusty said. "Clear out around the top of the structure there, lower a big collar over it, then a caisson around that. Pump water into the collar till it makes a seal, then pump the water outta the caisson."

"You've done that before?" Billy asked.

Rusty was a licensed salvor, as were his father and grandfather before him. He'd raised a lot of boats back up from the bottom after an inattentive captain had torn the hull open on the reef.

"Aw, hell no, bro," Rusty replied. "Seen it on *Discovery* once. Sub sank at the dock with nobody aboard to pump out the leaky ballast tank."

"How long would it take?" Billy asked, handing the can back to me and stepping back over to the roof of the conning tower.

Rusty shrugged. "I could probably conjure up the equipment in a week or two, and maybe another week to build the caisson around it."

"But it *is* possible?" Billy asked hopefully.

"That's just the easy part," Rusty replied. "With a caisson in place, it'd only take a coupla hours to pump the water out and expose the hatch."

He paused and scratched the back of his neck. "But gettin' the sub *outta* here? You're talkin' mountains of bureaucracy, probly years, if at all, then weeks or months of dredging to the nearest canal!"

He turned and looked back the way we'd come, shaking his head. "I don't think them canals was dug deep either. So then ya got more months of dredging the canals deeper. Likely they'd have to build a new flood control dam to act as a lock near an existing one, then tear the old one down and dredge more all the way to the coast and for a good mile offshore. It's fuckin' shallow out there *because* of the Glades, man! It's millions of years of uncontrolled runoff."

Billy stood and turned, gazing westward. "Remember that environmentalist guy about six or seven years ago? Blew up one of the flood control dams and tried to stop development of Cayo Costa."

"Breeze," Jimmy said. "Meade Breeze. What about him?"

"His idea was sound," Billy replied, continuing to stare out over the sawgrass. "The water being diverted to the sugar and orange crops—and to the millions of new people—comes from here. The River of Grass is going dry. Strangled by the advancement of civilization."

"What would anything he did change what we got here?" Rusty asked. "And how does it apply to this sub?"

Jimmy vaulted over the nearly submerged rail, landing in the water with a splash. Then he slowly stood up and felt around in front of his body as he shuffled his feet around.

"The forward rail is right here, man," he said, looking back at Billy. "Still intact! I barely feel any surface rust. And I can feel the hatch with my feet. It's closed. How far's the nearest canal?"

"You can't possibly be considering floating this thing out of here," I said. "That'd be a monumental task, even after all the red tape, which I don't think would get approved."

"Who said anything about permits and stuff?" Jimmy asked. "I think Breeze had the right idea, man. He just didn't think big enough. We blow three levees; the water here rises ten feet, and we only need to follow canals that are at least ten feet deep now."

"Even if you went through with it and re-flooded the Everglades," I said, not believing the craziness they were talking, "you'd still have to follow those *submerged* canals without the sawgrass to guide you, and which aren't marked."

Billy held up his phone. "Marking the waypoints is child's play."

"Still," I countered, "you have to *move* this thing to one of those canals,"

"Jesse, look," Billy said, pointing ahead of the sub. "I think we can do it. Either of our planes can land on that canal. We can pump out around the conning tower and get it open in a few weeks and inspect the inside. If it's as I think it will be, she might only need new batteries to get the electric motor going. Think about it. We might be able to drive a sub out of the Everglades."

Jimmy climbed up on the corner of the rail, knees braced against the top rail. "It's been sealed up all this time. It's very possible that the electrical is still a hundred percent, except the batteries, of course. We replace those, flip the 'on and off' switch or whatever, then follow the canals to the sea, where we blow the dam and float right through on a counter-surge."

"That'd be an '*ein* und *aus*' switch," I muttered. "Still you're talking about flying equipment in, manpower, and somehow dredging a ten-foot-deep, twenty-foot-wide canal for a quarter mile. Do you *really* think nobody will notice?"

"Nobody has noticed for *eighty* years," Billy countered. "This thing was here before any of us were born. Besides, it will give us something to do. We're not getting any younger either."

"Speaking of," I said, staring up at my oldest friend, "what was that shit Trish was saying about your eyes and night?"

Billy stepped back over to the airboat and sat on the gunwale. "I hoped you hadn't heard that," he said softly, eyes cast down at the deck. "I am going blind. A very slow process, but my doctor said that if I live long enough, I will one day be totally blind."

"What?" I asked, sitting in the end seat. "How long are we

talking here?"

He looked up and grinned. "He says that by the time I'm one hundred and thirty, my vision will be completely gone." He paused and looked around at all of us. "I don't see as well as I once did and that's most apparent at night."

"Can't they do nothin'?" Rusty asked.

"No," he replied. "I was diagnosed with advanced glaucoma. I put drops in my eyes twice a day to slow the progression, but nothing can stop it."

"So... at a hundred?" I asked.

He looked up. "I'll still be able to see that you are uglier than me."

"But no traipsin' through the woods after dark?" Rusty asked.

"It's difficult," Billy said. "It attacks the optic nerves of the peripheral vision first."

"And our peripheral vision is what we use most in the dark," Jimmy said, nodding. "You can't see a faint star if you look right at it. Only when you look slightly away."

"I know it sounds dumb," Billy said, "but I can see what I look at just fine. It's just a matter of knowing where something is for me to focus on." He paused and looked around at the three of us again. "Now, about this submarine I found."

"I'm in for whatever you want to do," Jimmy said, obviously excited.

"What you're talking about could get us life in prison, Jimmy," I reminded him. "For us three, that's not much of a deterrent, but you're only forty-four."

"Look," Rusty said, "crazy as it sounds, I'm in, too. If we open her up and find she's worth salvaging, we'll go from there. And if push comes to shove, I can bring my barge up here to dredge it out.

We can take turns working nights and stash the barge in deep water durin' the day by sinking it. It ain't like you and me ain't dredged without a permit before."

"Sink it?" Billy asked.

"Why not?" he responded, looking down at the water. "It hid this sub for eight decades. The backhoe on the barge is diesel and equipped with snorkels; it'll be fine as long as water don't get to the wiring in the dash or the battery. All that's above the seat." He looked around and then pointed to a very old, fallen cypress surrounded by red mangrove and a couple of sabal palms a few hundred yards ahead. "That's the hidin' spot, yonder. The barge can be flooded close to that stand, sinking it, and only the seat would be visible. Then pump the water out to float it again."

"You're talking about a shit-ton of work," I said. "That'd take months! Not to mention the commission of at least a few felonies!"

"Sounds like a great adventure, *mi capitan*," Jimmy said. "And I can help cover the cost too, thanks to those stones we found last spring."

"Whoa," I said. "You and Naomi were planning to use that to buy a house."

Jimmy climbed back over onto the airboat again, water dripping onto the deck from his soaked shorts. "If we could recover this thing *intact*, man, think of what it'd bring. I know a good deal when I see it, and if Billy's cutting us in, my share would be way more than what Dink and I split. And that's not even counting anything we might find *inside*." He glanced back at the conning tower. "And if Naomi and I have to live in the damned thing, well, it's gonna need a paint job, man."

Then he began singing the opening line of "Yellow Submarine."

"Hold up, hold up," Rusty said. "Since you brought it up, and there might be some financial gain here, before we do anything, we should make a pact."

"A pact?" Billy asked.

"How any gain will be split," Rusty said. "You found it, and you asked us for help, so you name the terms."

Billy looked around at the three of us. "I get half," he said. "Which will go to the Council for Indigenous Peoples' Studies."

The truth was, none of us *needed* the money, except maybe Jimmy. I didn't know how much he'd saved, but I knew that he'd lived frugally the whole time he'd worked for me and had intimated last summer that he was close to buying a house and paying cash.

I also knew how expensive homes were in the area.

Rusty was flush, having been a part of a number of treasure finds over the years. A few times with me. The Anchor was no longer the money pit his father had left him. He'd repaid what I'd invested years ago, and he and Sid were now sitting on a gold mine.

I enjoyed the satisfaction of knowing that my kids, their kids, and their kids' kids would never *have* to work. I also knew they probably would. It was in their DNA. So, Pap's legacy would probably extend far beyond my great-grandchildren. And we'd keep adding to it and paying it forward.

"I'm good with that," I said. "That is, *if* we decide to move forward after we open the hatch, and..." I looked around at the beauty surrounding us—old Florida, untouched by civilization—until my gaze met Billy's. "And considering where we are, I'll donate my share, too."

Billy nodded somberly.

"Same here," Rusty said. "Minus costs, of course."

"If it's minus what we pitch in," Jimmy said, "then my share can go to the CIPS too, man."

WAYNE STINNETT

"I think you're all nuts," I said. "But I'm okay with opening it up and examining the interior. We're going over to Stuart *this* weekend." I looked over at Billy. "If Rusty can get the equipment together, you and I can shuttle it out here next week or whenever he gets it."

I paused and looked around at all three of them. "But let's get something perfectly clear here. If we find human remains aboard when we open it up, everything stops, any investment we made is lost, and we close it back up. I won't be comfortable doing anything other than reporting it to the authorities. I'll cover all the costs, so nobody is at risk but me and my convictions. Is that agreed?"

All three nodded, and Rusty solidified it. "Enemy or not, the dead should be treated with respect."

CHAPTER TWELVE

In a small house on the western outskirts of Havana, two men sat on opposite sides of a table, reading. There was a single bare bulb hanging above the table, illuminating it and a small part of the sparsely furnished living room. Each man was bent over his work, and there were several stacks of papers in seemingly disorganized piles around them on the table.

One man was older than the other, but not elderly. He wore reading glasses as he ran a finger down a page, stopping occasionally to read an entry before moving on, and finally setting the page aside to pick up another.

"Here is something," the younger man said, looking up from a sheet of paper in his hands. "It describes the sighting of and the attack on a submarine north of the Windward Passage."

"Any identifying markings?" the other man asked.

"No, but the description fits the three-twenty."

"When?" the other man asked, still not looking up.

"The fifteenth of October, Karl," the first man said. "Just a few days before the mysterious radio message. This report from a naval destroyer says that a submarine was sighted on the surface heading south toward the Windward Passage and it was attacked with depth charges. Another entry, less than an hour later had it sighted again heading west-northwest. The destroyer gave chase for nearly one hundred miles, sighting it several more times before losing it in the Gulf Stream."

Karl finally looked up. "It headed *toward* America? Why do you think he would do that, Paul?"

"He did for at least two hundred kilometers," Paul replied. "Perhaps he thought doubling back would throw his pursuers off? I don't know."

Karl sat back, thinking. "By alternating electric and engine power, he could stay at sea for weeks at a time. Long enough to make detours for safety."

"A detour going all the way around Cuba?" Paul asked. "So close to America? That would add several hundred miles, not to mention the danger."

Karl made a dismissive wave. "German submarine crew members were able to go ashore in towns all along America's coasts during the war. Going against the current would make it more difficult for a surface craft to follow. The delay would be a couple of days at most. And they would not have been low on fuel; we know they met a bunker ship north of Bermuda. And all that is supposing that sighting was our sub."

Karl picked up a single sheet that was set apart from the others and scanned it again. It was a report from a radio operator in Nicaragua who'd picked up a transmission from a station in Cuba trying to reach a boat that was reporting being stranded somewhere west of Havana, having run from a massive storm at sea, which had finally driven their vessel far inland.

The report from the Nicaraguan listening station said that although *he* couldn't hear the stricken vessel, the Cuban station could, and it had been obvious that the original transmission had been in German and the caller had identified himself as the captain of U-320.

It made no sense. But it was the only clue they had after the submarine had refueled in the middle of the Atlantic and had then headed south toward its destination in Venezuela.

Karl and Paul, with the backing of friends in Europe and Cuba, had searched the coastline west of the capital city by air and sea, using sophisticated reconnaissance equipment that could "see" through the dense jungle and beneath the waves.

They had talked to people all along the island nation's north shore and had scoured the archives in Havana.

No German submarine had landed there in late 1944.

Two months earlier, the U.S. Naval Archives had released declassified documents about much of the war in the Atlantic, and it was those documents the two men had been examining for several weeks—tens of thousands of pages.

"Set that one aside," Karl said. "And let's go down and get a beer while we think it over."

The two men went down three flights of stairs and through the hostel's small reception area. Outside, they turned right, and, after a short walk, they arrived at a little cantina that served food.

"I still don't think it would have been wise to go through Florida Strait," Paul said, after they'd ordered something to eat. "Too dangerous."

"I have been thinking about that," Karl said, pulling a pen out and using a paper napkin to draw on. "This is Cuba," he said, drawing a long, roughly elliptical shape. "And here's Florida, Hispanola, and the coast of South America."

He drew two more shapes with a line across the bottom for the continent.

"Not very accurate," Paul said, taking a gulp from a large beer mug. "But yeah, okay."

"The coded radio transmission sent to the group in Venezuela said that they had passed through the Windward Passage the day before and had encountered enemy surface craft, had tried zigzagging to lose the attacker, and, after having a number of near misses from depth charges, were able to flee south underwater."

"I've read it a hundred times, Karl," Paul grumbled. "I can recite it word for word. They headed due south at top speed to try to outrun the surface vessel and when it was clear, they continued south toward Venezuela but never arrived."

Karl took another napkin and drew a long line with a squared off hook at the end, like the letter J.

"Exactly," he said. "Here's the path the report from the Nicaraguan listening station said he had understood the boat had sailed—south for four days, then west for a day to wait out an approaching storm, and finally turning north, running from a violent storm to seek shelter in deeper water."

"So?"

Karl laid the two napkins side by side, showing how close the sub had been to the Venezuelan coast when it had to change course for the storm.

"It doesn't explain how he was later near Havana," Karl said. "If I laid this over the other, would you agree the distances are roughly accurate?"

Paul nodded. "They couldn't have been more than a hundred miles out when the storm came off the coast."

Karl picked up the second napkin and turned it ninety degrees.

"What if their compass was damaged when they were depth-charged?"

"I don't get it," Paul said, leaning forward conspiratorially.

Karl lifted the napkin and placed it on top of the other, holding one corner down while he lifted and lowered the rest to see the crude map beneath.

Paul's eyes widened. "That would explain how he ended up in Havana. He sailed around the western tip of Cuba, thinking he was sailing south."

"But he didn't run aground near Havana," Karl said. "The report said he was driven far inland. Remember how high that shoreline is?"

Paul nodded. "Then if it wasn't Havana, where was it?"

"Suppose that the captain realized the malfunction after they'd run aground and based on where he *thought* he'd been during the attack, he assumed he'd sailed all the way around the western part of Cuba, just as you did, and was then driven ashore near Havana. He'd never been to Cuba, so wouldn't know the terrain at all."

Paul leaned over and looked at the crude drawings. "And that would also explain his radio message. But we've searched that whole area for months and others have searched hundreds of times over the years. Just based on the captain's garbled radio message. Personally, I think he was closer to Venezuela than anyone has guessed and when he skirted the coastline and turned north, had run aground on one of those dive destination islands—the ABCs."

Karl looked up at his partner and smiled. "I agree partly. I *also* think the captain was incorrect in his position when he radioed that he was through the Windward Passage several days earlier and was attacked."

"So, you're saying we should start looking there? Aruba?"

Karl shook his head. "We just don't know. But one thing I'm sure of—my grandfather didn't know where he was *either* of the times when he broke radio silence. If that report you found *was* the three-twenty, then he was far north of where he thought he was when he was attacked."

Paul's eyes got wider. "You think he headed through the Florida Strait, thinking he was already south of Cuba and still going south?"

Karl lifted the top napkin and placed it higher, so the course of the sub lay north of Cuba instead of south.

Karl looked up and arched an eyebrow. "What if he didn't go around *Cuba*, but blindly headed west-northwest and went around the Florida Keys instead?"

Then he lifted one corner and lowered it again.

The end of the hook that represented the sub's course ended off the coast of Southwest Florida.

Karl ran a finger over the longer line, the one that represented what he suspected his grandfather thought was a southerly course.

"Because he was steaming against the current this whole time, his distance would be less. Remember the report of the hurricane?"

Paul thought for a moment. "It was about that same time of year, wasn't it?"

"Nearly a week after the sub reported being attacked," Karl said, nodding. "Most who believe he sailed around Cuba believe it was that hurricane that drove him inland. What if they were steaming through the Florida Strait the whole four days when they thought they were heading south?"

Paul nodded with enthusiasm. "Yes, yes! Then he'd turned right for a day, trying to dodge a storm that was coming off what he thought was the South American coast, but was actually Cuba!"

Karl smiled again.

"And then he might have thought he could go north into deeper water and dive below the violence on the surface." Paul crumpled the top napkin and put a finger on a spot representing the Florida coast. "Only he couldn't dive, because the farther he went, the shallower it got." He stabbed the spot on the napkin again. "And he landed here, thinking he was near Havana after figuring out his compass was broken. But how could he be that far off in his reported location the previous week?"

The waitress brought their food and refilled their beer mugs, and Karl waited until she left, then leaned close to his partner. "Hurricanes are massive. If I remember correctly, and we should confirm this as soon as we return to the apartment, this storm formed several days before the radio message saying he'd escaped an attack and was four days out, and it sat unmoving for a couple of days just east of the Cayman Islands. A large storm like this could blanket most of the western part of the Caribbean, half the Gulf of Mexico, and most of Florida with a dense cloud cover, even as it was forming."

"They didn't have radar," Paul said, while chewing a bite of his dinner. "Maybe they couldn't get a reading on the sun and stars for a couple of days and were relying on dead reckoning. Your grandfather had never sailed down here; he was strictly in the North Sea and the English Channel, so might not know how strong the Gulf Stream is and figured he'd gone farther south than he really did."

Karl chewed thoughtfully. Finally, he placed his fork down and said, "I think we should continue our search in Florida."

CHAPTER THIRTEEN

When we got back to the fish camp, we were met at the dock by Billy's partner, or girlfriend, or whatever term is used these days to describe a man and woman cohabitating.

Trish Osceola was a strikingly beautiful woman, and obviously intelligent. That more than anything made the two of them a good fit. Billy seemed more relaxed than I'd seen him in years. I was happy for both of them.

Billy turned at an angle toward where she stood on the dock and cut the engine twenty feet away.

When I removed my headset, my ears were met by total silence as the airboat glided across the water, spinning slowly, without a sound.

Trish shielded the setting sun from her eyes as she looked up at Billy. "Were you able to get inside?"

"No," he replied. "They talked me out of it."

She fended the airboat away from the dock, then grabbed a line I handed her and pulled us up alongside it.

"But we're pretty sure it's a sub," Rusty said, tying off the stern line.

"And the entire hull is buried in muck twenty feet deep," I added.

Jimmy stepped over to the dock. "Cutting it open prematurely would ruin anything inside, since it'd take a long time to get it out of there."

"Get it..." Trish began, then looked up at Billy. "You want to recover the whole thing?"

I retrieved my go-bag from under the seat and joined them on the dock, looking at my three closest friends. "I think we all have a fascination with finding things and the adventure it brings. It's been a while since the four of us did anything together like we did today." Then I turned to Trish. "But what these guys have in mind is just nuts."

"No, it isn't." Billy jumped down to the dock and put his hands on Trish's waist. "Remember that dugout on display at the Calusa Museum?"

"Of course," she replied. "You found it."

"It was buried under five feet of mud," Billy said. "*Pa-hay-okee* mud—the botanical detritus of all living things for thousands of years, probably covered by the piles of sawgrass that are uprooted after every storm. With the wood deprived of oxygen, it didn't rot."

"And you think this submarine of yours didn't rust?"

"I *know* it didn't," Jimmy said. "There was hardly any surface rust on a handrail we tied off to. I've been around boats all my live. That rail would either have to have been submerged less than a year or so, or somehow preserved by the almost bentonite-like qualities of organic matter deposited over a long time."

"Are you a scientist?" Trish asked Jimmy.

The three of us laughed and Jimmy glared at us, reddening.

"Sorry, Jimmy," Rusty said, stepping over to the dock. "Lack of schoolin' aside, you're one of the smartest people I know."

Jimmy turned to Trish. "No, I'm not a scientist. More of what you might call an autodidact, ya know. I have a curious mind and remember everything."

"*And* he thinks he was a conquistador in a past life," Billy added, clapping Jimmy on the shoulder. "So, take most of what this guy says with a grain of salt." He paused. "But in this case, he is correct."

Billy turned and faced all of us. "I was thinking the same thing on the ride back. The decaying plants once covered even the top of the conning tower. As the water level drops, more will be exposed."

Jimmy nodded. "And the water once covered the organic soil— or muck—by as much as ten feet, man. That's one-third more atmosphere of pressure. Exposed, it's going to rust, and rust fast."

"Closer to thirty at the *bottom* of the hull," I added.

"Pressure," Billy added. "All the oxygen and eventually the water would leach from the organic material and mud, so there would be no anaerobic bacteria either."

"No oxygen—no rust," Jimmy said. "Doesn't take a PhD to know that."

Trish looked around at all of us. "It is possible to get it out, then?"

"No," I said, scanning the area around the dock. We were completely alone. "No *legal* way."

"What does that mean?"

Rusty pulled his go-bag out of the boat and turned to Trish. "Means your 'boyfriend' and the 'autodidact' here are thinkin' of blowin' up Flood Control."

"You said you were in, man," Jimmy complained.

"I am," Rusty said, then turned to Billy. "And you wasn't the only one ponderin' on the ride back. To do it right, you're gonna need a civil engineer who specializes in hydrology. Otherwise, a bunch of people are gonna get flooded outta their homes and the sub's still gonna be stuck, if not lost completely. Prolly need a mechanical engineer and somebody familiar with antique submarines. We need to go to your place for a serious powwow."

"Did he just say—"

"Ignore him," Billy said to Trish. "He doesn't mean anything by it, but he's right. We need to sit down and put our heads together; do some research."

Trish glanced quickly back toward the building. "Lem can run things. I'm coming. You bunch of knuckle-draggers need guidance."

I laughed. "I think she and Savvy will get along fine."

"And Savvy is?"

"My wife," I replied. "She and Jimmy's fiancée, Naomi, are probably at Billy's house now."

"Then let's get going," Trish said, taking Billy's arm and turning him toward the foot of the dock. "I'll duck in and let Lem know we're leaving and to hose down and refuel your boat."

We fell in behind them, and I couldn't help but think she was exactly the kind of efficient, no-nonsense woman Billy needed in his life.

Fifteen minutes later, we pulled into Billy's yard and found the Camaro parked where it had been earlier, with the top up.

"I don't see any visible damage," I said.

"She really that rough on cars, man?" Jimmy asked. "It never occurred to me that she didn't have a lot of experience behind the wheel."

"Oh, she's got plenty of experience," I said. "Just not much recently. Besides running one of her dad's shrimp boats, she used to drive the refrigerator truck to fish markets all up and down coastal Georgia and South Carolina. She just has... sort of a lead foot, I guess."

The screen door opened as we were climbing out of the huge Excursion, and Savannah stepped out onto the porch.

"Just in time," she said, as Alberto came out behind her. "We were getting hungry. Is there a good restaurant nearby?"

"Billy's Shack is close," Trish said, stepping up to the porch. "I am Trish Osceola. You must be Savvy."

Savannah stepped down off the porch and shook her hand. "Yes, I am."

"Billy and I live together," Trish said. "Mostly at my home in Buckhead Ridge."

I could see the surprise in her eyes as she glanced at Billy, then me, but she recovered quickly. "Very nice to meet you, Trish. Now, what's 'Billy's Shack?'"

"It is my kitchen in the backyard," Billy said. "Is beef okay with everyone?"

"Beef?" Alberto asked. "You mean like steak?"

Billy nodded at Alberto. "The best Angus available. I can make yours a steak, or I can let you grind it to make your own burger. How's that?"

"Really?"

"Why not?" Billy said. "Best burger you'll find."

"An outdoor kitchen?" Savannah asked. "We don't eat much beef on the island, but we do eat outdoors a lot. So yes, that would be a treat."

"Drop your bag in the house," Billy said to me. "Nothing is needed from the inside kitchen, and there is plenty of seating on the deck for everyone. We can talk there while the potatoes are baking."

The deck behind Billy's house had been a small thing when we were kids. Leaping Panther had built it when he'd first bought the place in the 1960s.

The outdoor kitchen had been Billy's first addition, set well away from the old deck. Over the years, the deck grew in tiers, and the kitchen became a part of it—a long-range vision Billy'd had and slowly implemented. But he'd wanted the kitchen first.

"Everyone, sit," Billy said, waving his hand toward a large fire pit built into the lower level of the deck.

As we all took our seats around the dormant fire pit, Trish moved to a large commercial refrigerator. "Okay, so start from the beginning," she said, taking a tray out and placing it on a counter.

"We found it fairly easily," Billy said, opening a stainless-steel cover on a large rotisserie grill. "Thanks to Jimmy's sharp eyes."

He put a dozen large potatoes and some unshucked corn cobs on the trays of the rotisserie, then closed it and flipped a switch on.

"Then Jesse used a telescoping baton," Billy continued. "And he was able to reach through the mud and we could hear the ring of metal on metal about seven or eight feet down."

"Why is that important?" Naomi asked.

"For one thing," Jimmy replied, "it tells us we're dealing with a full-sized submarine, not a mini-sub with a two-foot conning tower."

"Based on the shape of the superstructure and its height above the hull," I said, "I think it's safe to say it's at least a hundred feet long, probably twice that."

"What did the top look like?" Alberto asked, looking down at his tablet.

"Higher behind the flybridge deck," Billy replied. "Why do you want to know?"

Alberto turned his tablet around to show silhouettes of different kinds of warplanes used during WWII. "They used to have coast watches here and in England," he replied. "They had these drawings to identify different kinds of airplanes." He paused and swiped the screen. "And even submarines."

Jimmy leaned over and looked closer, then pointed a finger. "We could only see a couple feet of the top—that water's wicked dark, man. But this one looks like it."

"That's a German U-boat," Alberto said, reading the screen. "It's a VIIC/41, whatever that means."

"The design model," I said, also leaning over for a closer look. "Can you—"

"Here it is," he said. "First built in 1943, there were only ninety-one of them completed."

"Only ninety-one?" Trish asked, amazed. "They had more than that of another model or something?"

"During the war," Jimmy replied, "Germany built over a thousand subs. What made this model so special that they only built a relatively few of them?"

Alberto looked up from his tablet. "What's a crush depth?"

"The limit that a sub can go," Jimmy replied. "Usually an estimate, of course."

"It says it has a reinforced hull," Alberto said, reading from the tablet. "And lighter on-board equipment, so it can go deeper and faster, down to almost a thousand feet! But it was only tested at seven hundred and fifty. That's still pretty deep."

Jimmy let out a whistle. "Twenty-four atmospheres of pressure. I don't think thirty feet of mud would compromise that hull." He paused and grinned. "It'd be cool to go down and see the Gulf Stream from the bottom, man."

Alberto looked up from his tablet at all of us. "It says there's only one of this kind still in existence."

"Now there are two," Billy said. "If that's the kind that's out there."

"That'd make this thing pretty danged valuable," Rusty said. "I remember a demilitarized Brit sub from that time selling in an auction a few years back for over two million bucks."

"If Rusty and Jimmy's hypothesis is correct," I said, looking around the table, "and it's really the only plausible way a sub like that could be where it is, then we at least know *when* it got there—October the nineteenth, 1944."

Rusty noted a couple of incomprehensive looks from Trish and Naomi. "He's talkin' about the Cuba-Florida Hurricane of 1944," he explained. "Crossed western Cuba as a Cat Four and made landfall near Sanibel Island on that date. We figure the only way a sub could be that far inland was because it was caught up in a hurricane's tidal surge and that was the only landfallin' 'cane in that area durin' the whole war."

"Four months *after* D-Day and the liberation of France," Jimmy said. "The writing was on the wall, man. Upper echelons in Germany's army and navy were in turmoil. Rats running from a sinking ship. Hitler was hiding in a bunker. A lot of Nazi generals and admirals escaped to South America as the Third Reich fell."

"It sounds to me like this is a very valuable find," Trish said, looking around the table.

"If we can recover *anything*," Billy said, "the proceeds will go to the Council."

She looked around at the others, surprised.

"What council?" Savannah asked.

"The Council for Indigenous Peoples' Studies," I replied. "Billy and Trish met at the conference in Brazil."

"Oh," Savannah said. "That's good, then."

"We actually met long before that," Trish said, smiling at Billy.

"Oh?" Naomi said. "How did you two meet?"

"I've known Billy all my life," she replied. "As most of our people have. He was ten, working in a daycare at a tribal conference and I wasn't even walking. One of the elder women told my mother that Billy had me taking my first steps that weekend."

"There are only two thousand of our people," Billy said. "So we are a part of each other's lives."

"There is one stipulation," Rusty said. "And we all agreed on this. When we open it up in a week or so, if we find anyone... you know... *still aboard*, we turn the find over to the authorities."

"I'm sure glad y'all decide dat," Naomi said, falling into full blown Cajun. "Don't want no *feu-follet* chasing me 'round for eternity."

Several laughed and Trish nodded. "I agree. I would not wish to disturb the dead."

"What else can you find on that thing, Alberto?" Rusty asked. "Like how big is it? What's the draft? Overall height'd be good to know. And the tonnage? Dimensions of the conning tower would be excellent."

Alberto tapped on his screen a few times, then began to read. "They were 220 feet long, had a draft of fifteen feet, seven inches, and the height was thirty-one feet, six inches."

"About what we figured," Jimmy said. "With a foot and a half above the water, the keel's about thirty feet down in the muck."

"They displaced 860 tons, submerged," Alberto added.

"Geez," Rusty moaned, dropping his chin onto his hands and resting them on the table. "Might as well say a thousand tons with all the mud on her."

"Make that fifty of the world's biggest heavy-lift helicopters," I said. "You're not going to raise it."

"When I was a girl," Savannah said, "we used to go all around the sea islands in small boats, and sometimes we ended up on the wrong side of a low bridge due to the tide," She paused and turned to Trish. "It rises and falls up to eight or ten feet where I'm from, twice a day. But if we got stuck on the wrong side, we all knew that since we couldn't raise the bridge, we just had to wait for the tide to lower the river."

"You mean we should raise the water around the submarine?" Trish asked. "And what? Float it out of Everglades National Park? Just how do you plan to do that?"

I snapped my fingers and pointed at her. "And that's the *illegal* method I mentioned earlier."

CHAPTER FOURTEEN

The next morning over coffee, Rusty asked if I'd mind coming back through LaBelle on the way home. He and Jimmy were going to stay over and do more research and line up equipment.

"You're not planning on moving your dredging barge up here, are you?" I asked him.

"That's an ongoin' but yet-to-be-implemented part of the plan, for now. But first I gotta get a caisson and collar big enough, and that might take some doin'."

We said our goodbyes after breakfast, and Billy drove us out to the airport in his Camaro.

As we turned onto the highway, he looked back over his shoulder at Savannah. "Will the law be looking for my car?"

"No, but if you come across a teenage boy in a Challenger and he asks for a rematch, race him for pink slips."

"Pinks?" Billy said, seeming surprised by Savannah's use of the antiquated street racing term. "Car titles haven't been pink in a long time, and besides, I don't bet on anything I didn't build."

Thirty minutes later, Savannah, Alberto, and I were in the air for the short hop over to Stuart.

"Rusty seemed excited about what Billy found," Savannah said, when we got to cruising altitude and I let her take the yoke. "Are you certain it's a submarine?"

"Very," I replied with a chuckle. "And why wouldn't he be excited? I mean, a lost Nazi submarine doesn't turn up in the Glades very often."

She glanced over and smiled at me. "I think it's good, the four of you getting together on something. Even if it is a little whacky."

"Whacky?"

"Crazy, zany, fun... You're always so... I don't know."

"Uptight?"

"You said it. Not me."

"You are uptight a lot, Dad," Alberto echoed.

Savannah didn't get to fly very long. An hour after taking off, we were back on the ground at an airfield just blocks from the boatyard.

As soon as I set the brakes, I texted Hank Murphy, the project manager on our boat build, and told him that we'd arrived.

Savannah and Alberto went into the general aviation building while I went through the postflight, then went inside to the desk and arranged for fuel.

"Jesse!" a voice called.

I turned to see Hank coming toward me from the entrance.

"I thought you were bringing the family," he said, pumping my hand.

Savannah and Alberto came up behind him, returning from the restrooms. "He did," she said.

"Great!" Hank exclaimed. "I have a car waiting outside."

In minutes, we were whisked away to the boatyard in a town car.

"We've made a lot of progress since you were last here," Hank said, leaning over the back of the seat. "I think you will all be very impressed."

Just a few blocks later, the car pulled up in front of a huge metal building that could probably have covered half my island.

"Both amas have been joined to the main hull," Hank said, leading the way through the offices to the production facility in back and turning to talk to Savannah. "My last report to Jesse was that only one had been joined. And since they're smaller and more modular, with less wiring and plumbing involved, separate teams finished them well ahead of the main hull."

"How strong are these joints?" Savannah asked.

Hank grinned. "They were tested and withstood greater forces than you will *ever* encounter at sea. I know how unforgiving the sea can be, trust me, but Mother Ocean isn't nearly as taxing as a hydraulic ram."

When he opened the door at the end of the hall and we stepped through it, I was shocked. The boat looked massive. And it was.

With the outer hulls joined, it had a beam width of thirty feet, and the main hull's length was sixty-six feet, which included a long, slender, wave-piercing bow section.

Even without the cabin roof and flybridge it towered fifteen feet over our heads.

"Whoa," Alberto said, breathing the word out, as he too, skidded to a halt.

"It looks bigger," Savannah said. "All boats look bigger on the hard, though. I guess this would be our perspective in neck-deep water."

"That'd be about right," I said, noting that the main hull's keel was resting on blocks.

"Yes, that's a pretty good estimate," Hank said, leading us toward the stern of the boat. "The design draft is four feet, as Jesse specified."

Savannah ran a hand lightly along the surface of the starboard ama's hull. "It looks like... well, like nothing I've ever seen before. Futuristic, and yet elegant and refined at the same time."

"What are you doing, son?" I called back to Alberto.

"Taking a picture," he replied, standing twenty feet in front of the protruding bow section.

He ran toward us and showed Savannah the picture. "It looks like a giant osprey!"

"Yes, it does," she replied, as we climbed a set of stairs to a large, raised platform constructed at deck level with the bottom of the sugar scoop steps in each hull.

Alberto showed me his phone, and from the perspective the picture was taken, with only the main hull and the arms out to the amas visible, it did look like a giant bird of prey, swooping low and about to grab an unsuspecting fish.

On the large, temporary platform, there were different prefabricated interior parts and boxes of wiring, hoses, and electronic equipment stacked neatly along the back rail, waiting to be installed. The stairs in the main hull's sugar scoop were wide enough for two people to ascend side by side without crowding.

"Shall we start with the garage?" Hank asked. "This is my favorite part. And it's almost complete. We're just waiting for the tender you ordered to arrive so we can adjust the rollers."

"A custom tender?" Savannah asked.

Hank took a key fob from his pocket and handed it to me. "Press and hold the middle red button."

I did and heard the instant, barely audible whine of a hydraulic motor deep inside the boat. The whole set of steps began to rise.

"Not a custom tender," I told Savannah. "A custom-built yacht with a garage that was designed to just barely fit a production tender."

"Wow!" Alberto exclaimed, as the hatch rose and the inside light came on.

"You can't actually drive it in," Hank said. "But any twelve-foot tender with a jet-drive type of inboard propulsion will fit in there."

"The one I ordered is a diesel," I said. "Yanmar thirty-five horse. It has a stubby little windshield, but the overall height is four inches less than we have in there, with two inches on either side."

"What's under the other steps?" Alberto asked, pointing to the stern of the port ama.

"Huge lazarette storage or crew quarters," Hank replied. "But your dad had some specific plans for both. They also provide access to the wing motors."

We walked over to the port ama, and Hank continued. "Both are operated from individual control panels inside here," he said, opening a small hatch on the inside of the port hull's stairwell. "There's a fresh-water rinse hose at all three sugar scoops, as well."

He pushed a red button on the inside panel and the stairs began to rise, but unlike the main hull's garage door, which was just above the waterline, this one started opening from the third step up and three feet of the deck came up as well.

"You can also use the key fob to open and close the ama scoops," Hank said, stepping up to the third step, then descending a vertical ladder into the storage area. He stepped off the ladder and moved forward a few feet. "I'm standing on the motor's cover here, which would be a bed if this were crew quarters."

I turned to Alberto. "Instead, there will be racks for storing four kayaks and four paddle boards on this side, along with fenders and dock lines and a large deep freezer for all the fish we'll catch."

"Over to the starboard ama," Hank said, waving an arm and backtracking across the wide cockpit deck above. "Jesse, would you do the honors?"

I raised the hatch on the other side with the key fob and Hank said, "In here we've installed basically a full-on dive operation, complete with air and nitrox compressors, storage for up to twelve tanks, rebreather equipment, and a solar and battery-powered hookah rig. You will be able to outfit eight scuba divers, four rebreather divers, and four hookah divers who could go down to thirty feet, or two to sixty feet, or could reach the entire hull area for cleaning, but the hookah won't provide enough air pressure to dive more than sixty feet down."

I climbed up the steps and descended the ladder, then stepped down off the motor cover.

"This is perfect," I said, turning back to Savannah. "Compressor and controls all inboard to minimize distance to the electrical systems, with storage outboard and easy to get to."

"Where's my room?" Alberto asked.

"If you'll push the middle green button, Jesse," Hank said.

I held the button on the key fob and the large garage hatch began to lower, the joints matching perfectly once it latched into place.

Hank waved an arm. "Come on up to the cockpit, then."

We went up the steps to the main deck in the cockpit, which extended out over both amas to spacious and covered side decks. They were flush with the cockpit but rose two steps on either side, once you got up beyond the wheelhouse hatches.

The cockpit deck was also flush all the way through the galley, salon, and the main wheelhouse.

"You'll have a small outdoor dining area here," Hank said, pointing to an area on the port side, just aft the wide opening to the interior. "The entire width of the cockpit and interior dining area will be separated by polycarbonate glass door panels that open fully to a larger adjoining dinette. All four panels will slide back behind this bulkhead below where the flybridge steps will be, opening the cockpit to the salon area for maximum seating."

Savannah moved inside. The unfinished dinette and galley were to port, with a large seating area beyond that. To starboard was a recessed area for a full-sized refrigerator and freezer and several cabinets, and then the bulkhead continued the length of the room.

"You'll have a large flat-screen on the bulkhead here between the salon area and the master stateroom

Savannah turned to Hank, surprised. "The master's on the main deck?"

"The bed is four steps from the helm," Hank said. "I love this. It brings 'hot bunking' to a whole new dimension for a cruising couple."

Savannah hurried through the salon to the unfinished helm area and opened the diagonal hatch to the master stateroom.

"Oh, my..."

Four feet in along the inboard bulkhead was the platform for a king-sized bed, with room to walk all the way around it on the outboard side, which was a wall of glass.

"That is going to be an incredible view," Hank said. "It won't matter if it's day or night, good weather or bad, at sea or at the dock, that view will be off the hook."

I stepped into the room and stood by the bed platform, looking out through the tinted glass, then turned my head and looked through the hatch and windshield. "The view from two fathoms above sea level."

I turned to Savannah and pulled her toward the raised platform.

"Sit here," I said, turning her toward the hatch.

She sat down, and I pointed forward, through the hatch. "Your head right now is at the level it will be when you're lying on this bed, once the mattress is installed."

"I can see the pulpit over the helm," she said, amazed. "No more cramped couch during night passages?"

"Luxury hot bunking," I said. "You said you wanted the ultimate trawler."

"This platform," Hank said, "and the one on the opposite side where the raised dinette is, are actually the overheads of the two sides of the mechanical room below deck."

"Where's my room?" Alberto asked again.

"Port side," I replied. "Forward or aft. Take your pick."

"There's a guest room?" Savannah asked.

I held up a peace sign. "Two, besides Alberto's."

I started to follow after our son, toward the helm and seating area.

"Is it okay to go down there?" I asked Hank.

"Still doing a ton of wiring," he replied, "but we have LED lighting installed on motion sensors."

"I like that idea," I said. "Can they be incorporated into daylight sensors?"

He smiled. "Yes, sir. And I agree. In darkened areas like this companionway, or even as deck lighting in the cabins, I think having lights come on when you enter or get out of bed would be a nice touch."

"Make it happen," I told him, then started to turn toward the dark companionway leading down to the lower deck.

Savannah took my arm, stopping me. "What's in the other hull?"

"*Ama*," I corrected her. "It's what the Polynesians called the two outriggers on their fishing and trading canoes. The starboard ama is our head."

"That's it?" she asked, moving back into the stateroom. "Can we look?"

"The amas are supposed to be ahead of the main hull," I said, following her. "Closer to completion."

When her foot hit the first step, low-level, blue accent lights illuminated the the rest of the treads.

"Son-of-a..." I started to say, as Hank came back in. "You already did it."

"It's practically a requirement these days," Hank said. "Go ahead and look around down there. I'll go see if your son has decided, and maybe I can show him some features that will sway his decision."

Hank disappeared again and I could hear him calling out for Alberto as I followed Savannah down into the starboard ama.

"What do you think?" I asked when she reached the bottom and the lights came on.

She turned toward the bow and gasped, her eyes going wide and her hands covering her mouth.

CHAPTER FIFTEEN

By mid-morning the next day, Karl had found another report from an American Coast Guard cutter that had reported sighting a submarine on the surface about twenty miles west-southwest of the Dry Tortugas, heading almost due north before submerging. They'd been returning to Key West in heavy seas when they'd sighted it.

The date and time stamp on the report showed that the sighting had been in the late evening of October 18, 1944.

The same day the powerful hurricane had made landfall in western Cuba. Paul had been researching the stories in newspaper archives, and they were compiling more information on the hurricane.

The report from the cutter reinforced Karl's idea that the submarine had suffered damage or a malfunction to its navigation equipment, and was way off course and nowhere near where his grandfather had said they'd been when he reported being driven ashore.

"Here's another one," Paul said, handing Karl a sheet of paper with another latitude and longitude written on it. "The report is from a survivor near the town of Carnestown, who said his entire first floor was underwater."

Karl entered the coordinates into his terrain-mapping software.

"This is brilliant," Paul continued, leaning over the table. "By finding eyewitness reports and figuring out where the person was, it looks like the data we're compiling doesn't support where the news of the time said the storm made landfall."

Karl looked up from the screen. "The elevation at that location is six meters above sea level."

"Add another three for the height of the first floor," Paul said, looking down at the paper in his hand. "Even if it were built at ground level, that's a nine-meter surge, and farther south than where the reported landfall was. If we assume he exaggerated a little, we can call it eight meters." Paul looked up at Karl. "And this town is more than ten kilometers from the sea."

"Nine-point-three," Karl said, looking up and meeting the younger man's gaze. "From the nearest shoreline to these coordinates."

"If a tree falls in the forest and nobody is there to hear it?" Paul asked, then came around the table and pointed at the map. "There isn't anything there."

"Reports from the larger settlements along the coast," Karl said, as he turned and looked out the window, "from those towns where they *thought* it made landfall, all said it was a Category-2 storm, with a five-foot surge—less than two meters, barely enough to push a fishing boat onto the barrier islands."

Paul thought for a moment. "Could it have been an American sub?"

Karl shook his head. "Even a low-ranking Coast Guard crewman would be able to tell an American submarine from a German one. By late 1944, nearly all of Germany's were called back to protect the North Atlantic. There should have been no other in the Caribbean."

"I'm beginning to think your idea was correct," Paul said. "They'd misjudged their location *and* heading—sailing against the Gulf Stream north of Cuba."

"All other things being the same," Karl said, returning to his navigation map. He'd overlain the reported course and steaming time onto a nautical chart and could turn the course image any way he wanted.

"If their compass was off by something like ninety degrees," Karl said, turning the course image, "then they would have sailed west-northwest for four days, thinking they were going south-southwest toward Venezuela."

"And if they turned, thinking they were headed west off the South American coast, they'd actually be headed north, well west of Cuba."

He had to admit, the course lined up perfectly, starting where his grandfather had reported they'd passed through the Windward Passage and ending on the northern coast of Cuba, just southwest of Havana.

"And then due east," Karl said, looking at the end of the course line where his grandfather had reported they'd grounded.

Karl slowly moved the course line up the chart. "But if he was *wrong* about his initial location and the first report of the depth charge attack *south* of the Windward Passage..." Karl positioned the course line so that it started at the spot where the American vessel had reported attacking a submarine. "And he was actually *north* of the passage, the U-320 would have gone blindly through the narrow straight at over a hundred meters."

"And it ends in the middle of the Gulf of Mexico," Paul said.

"But the current is stronger there!" Karl exclaimed, knowing that he was right. "They were going against the current for four days. How much shorter would that long leg be?"

"Hang on...."

Paul went back to his laptop, typing in numbers on his phone's calculator as he sat down. "They said they steamed south at an average four knots, only surfacing long enough to run the engines and recharge the batteries. If they were in the Gulf Stream, the distance they'd travel in four days would be much less."

"How much?" Karl asked again.

Paul looked up. "Sixty percent at best."

Karl shortened the longest part of the course line by sixty percent, then adjusted it so that it missed all landmasses.

The starting position was almost exactly where the Americans had reported the sighting and the end of the hook, representing where the sub might be located, was very near the coast of Southwest Florida.

"They thought they were turning north toward deeper water," Karl said.

Paul came around the table again and looked at the map on Karl's computer screen. "Only it kept getting shallower as the storm was raging on the surface."

"And then driven inland," Karl said, his words soft. "Carried over the low barrier islands by the storm surge somewhere south of Marco Island. Grandfather had realized his navigation error and assumed he'd sailed around Cuba to land on the north coast."

"But he didn't realize his initial location error," Paul said. "He thought he was through the passage but was still on the north side. We need to go to Florida, Karl."

The older man stared at the screen. "But how could a sixty-seven-meter submarine go undiscovered for nearly eighty years?"

WEIGH ANCHOR

The satellite phone on the desk rang.

Paul picked it up and read the display. "It's Gupta."

Karl took the phone and tapped the *Accept* button, then held it to his ear. "Manish, I think we're onto something."

"Someone else is, also."

CHAPTER SIXTEEN

When I reached the lower deck in the ama, Savannah was already headed toward the custom-built shower enclosure.

She stopped next to it and looked back at me. "This is decadent, Jesse!"

I followed her forward to the large shower stall. It was simply a clear polycarbonate tube, with a diameter of six feet, extending from deck to overhead. An opening section of curved glass rolled on tracks and sealed with a rubber gasket when closed.

She slid the door sideways and it slid silently, following the contour of the tube enclosure.

"It doubles as a sauna," I told her, pointing out the controls on the outside.

"Get out!"

"Teak bench seating for two."

"Now you're just spoiling me," she said, stepping in and doing a pirouette with her arms outstretched.

"What's one of the hardest parts of long-distance cruising?" I asked her. "I mean from a personal point of view."

She looked back at the way we'd come.

"Never enough clothes," she said, stepping around me and opening the first of four double-door hanging lockers. "Are these all for clothes?"

"They can be," I replied. "And there are two more just like this in the aft section."

She looked around more slowly, taking it all in. Almost everything was installed, and the finish work was immaculate, including an electric flush toilet, double porcelain sinks set in a faux granite countertop, and a small bench with a window above it. With the other two hanging lockers aft and a double chest of drawers at the end, wardrobe wasn't going to be a problem.

"I love it so far," she said. "Let's go see what Alberto thinks."

We hurried up the companionway and then down the other one on the port side.

"I think I want the front one," Alberto said, coming toward us in the narrow passageway.

I'd designed the two cabins to be almost identical and was curious to know which subtle difference had swayed him. "Why the forward cabin?"

"There's more room between the hulls up there," he said, as if that explained everything. "You know, to watch dolphins."

Both cabins had rectangular outboard- *and* inboard-facing portholes, but he was right; the one in the forward cabin probably had two more feet between it and the main hull, which tapered like a knife blade to the bow.

"So the aft cabin will be fitted out as guest quarters, Hank," I told the project manager, winking. "And the forward cabin is to be fitted out for the first mate."

"Really?" Alberto asked.

"I think he's earned it," I said, turning to Savannah. "Don't you?"

"Oh, absolutely," she said. "That means no more mid-watch for me."

"The day head is here in this side," Hank said, opening a hatch. "It can also be accessed through the forward—er, first mate's cabin."

As we went back up, I stopped and showed Savannah and Alberto the one-piece sliding hatch that pulled out and covered the companionway's top and front.

"The recess it slides into is below the corner of the galley countertop." I said, opening a cabinet in the stairwell to reveal a small linen closet. "We could have put a lazy Susan there, but the galley already has tons of cabinets, so I thought the corner space could be better used to store towels and linens with easy access while the privacy hatch is closed."

"Shall we go to the lower deck?" Hank asked. "I think you're going to like what's down there, Alberto."

We went down the forward companionway, which curved ninety degrees to the left, and ended in a short centerline passageway.

"This is the laundry," Hank explained, theatrically opening the hatch to the right. "A commercial-sized front-loading washer and dryer will go here."

Savannah smiled. "For those *really* long passages where we run out of clothes."

"With the storage this boat has," Hank said, "that'd have to be exceptionally long."

"I want to go to *all* the ends of the Earth," Savannah said.

"This will be our home away from home," I said, taking her hand in mine. "Everything you'd want or need, except land."

"They're not in yet?" Savannah asked, leaning into the washer and dryer space.

Hank pointed up, inside the closet. "It's open all the way to the flybridge deck and there will be a large deck hatch below the sliding sunroof over the flybridge helm. Just about everything on this deck will fit through the hatch, if and when something needs to be replaced."

"Except the main engine," I said. "The deck directly above it in the salon opens up, and there's an eight-foot deck hatch up on the top deck."

"You two really have thought of everything," Savannah said.

Hank turned and went forward, opening the hatch at the end of the passageway.

"The VIP stateroom," he announced. "It will have a full head and separate shower to port, a walk-in closet to starboard, and a queen centerline berth with tons of storage underneath."

"Wow!" Savannah said, stepping into the room. "I had no idea there would be so much room down here."

"Forward is even more storage," Hank said. "All accessed through deck hatches in all three hulls' wave-piercing bow sections. Each bow section is separated from the rest of its hull by watertight bulkheads. A truly *massive* amount of deck storage in those."

"What's through there?" Alberto asked, pointing back down the passageway.

"I understand you have a very sharp mind," Hank said. "That's the part I think you're going to like—the mechanical room. Much more than just an engine room, though that's where the main engine is located, but also all the other mechanical components. They're still working on plumbing and wiring, so please watch your step when we go in there."

We moved aft and Hank undogged the heavy steel door. "The entire mechanical room is incapsulated in sound-deadening insulation and steel-reinforced carbon fiber with titanium structural beams, supports, and crossmembers. It is air-conditioned, and combustion air for the engine and generators is drawn from air intakes just under the overhangs on either side deck."

"Sounds heavy," Savannah said, following Hank in. "Even with the lighter metals."

"It is," Hank replied. "But surprisingly, not heavy enough. There's more than a thousand pounds of steel ballast in the keel below the engine, and a twenty-two-hundred-pound gyrostabilizer under the deck just inside the door here."

We followed him in and were able to spread out, stepping over rolls of wire where necessary, but it wasn't cramped at all, and I'm six-three.

In the center was the main engine, a Caterpillar C-8.7, rated at a whopping 650 horsepower. The gleaming yellow engine was surrounded by a matching yellow, two-inch tubular aluminum railing.

"The weight is concentrated here by design," Hank continued. "The mechanical room is the lowest part of the boat and acts as a ballast, with more than sixty percent of the gross tonnage being in this one compartment. All the air conditioning, hydraulics, batteries, fuel and water tanks, reverse osmosis, generators... *All* the mechanical parts are right here."

Savannah pointed at the coolant hoses, disappearing through the deck. "No heat exchangers to replace?"

"Closed loop cooling," I replied. "The coolant passes through tubes built into the steel ballast in the keel. Once every couple of years, we'll have to pull the caps off the bottom to inspect the plumbing and replace the sealant around it. But that's it—no more rusty heat exchangers."

"How fast will she go?" Savannah asked, pointing at the big yellow beast. "That's a lot of engine."

"Running on the outer hulls' electric motors only, and at a speed that will still allow the solar generation to be more than the demand, you could cruise at three and a half knots indefinitely."

"Indefinitely?" Savannah asked, raising an eyebrow. "Even at night?"

"By keeping the electrical demand at less than half of what is generated by the rooftop solar panels, they will not only be able to power the boat, but charge the batteries throughout the day, and then use that stored energy all night. Clouds permitting, of course."

"And if we need to go faster than that," I said, patting one of two built-in gen-sets, "this is a dedicated diesel generator for the electric motors in the amas. It'll come on when *their* dedicated batteries get to fifty percent. Cruising speed on generator-powered electric should be about twelve knots, with a fifty-fifty run time on the gen-set."

"And with that," she said, once more pointing to the main engine.

Both engines in Savannah's trawler combined didn't produce as much horsepower as the Cat, and they used about the same amount of fuel, if not more.

I'd designed and was building an exploration vessel that could go for months without visiting a dock or town, and if I wanted it to, the boat could cross any ocean using only the power of the sun and wind.

I'd tried to think globally. I really had. But according to my wife, I'm a knuckle-dragging Neanderthal—which I don't completely disagree with—and dammit, I wanted more power and speed.

I shrugged. "Better to have it and not need it than need it and not have it. If a sudden hurricane was bearing down on us at twenty knots, we could fire up the Cat here, and run away from it at thirty."

"Thirty *knots*?" she asked. "This whole thing? Or just the escape pod attached to the bottom?"

"*That's* still on backorder," I said grinning. "But did I mention we can also go kite flying?"

CHAPTER SEVENTEEN

With the tour of the inside complete, we went back up to the wheelhouse and then out the port-side hatch and up to the long foredeck.

Immediately in front of the main house was a slightly elevated area where a sun pad would go, large enough for a Roman orgy. In front of it would be seating for five people.

Temporary pole-and-cable safety rails ran forward on both sides to the pulpit, at the end of an ever-narrowing deck. Finished, they'd be replaced with polished aluminum rails.

"Are you planning to do a lot of entertaining?" Savannah asked, as Alberto walked all the way out to the end of the bow. "Four staterooms and no crew quarters?"

I pointed forward. "That whole bow section can easily be crew quarters if a time comes that we want a crew," I replied. "Right now, it's just extra storage. We have room for four guests in two staterooms, or ten in a pinch, if we lower the dinette table, convert the lounge seating, Alberto doubles up, and someone sleeps on the couch. You know, in case *all* the kids want to spend some time with us in the Greek Islands."

"The Greek Islands?" she asked, arching an eyebrow. "I thought you were strictly a Caribbean sailor."

"Item number twelve on my bucket list," I replied. "Climb Mount Olympus and dwell amongst the gods."

She laughed.

"Wherever we go," I continued, "if they all want to come at the same time, we have room."

"That'd be all ten of us," Alberto shouted exuberantly as he strode back from the bow. "*Fire!*"

"Cool," Savannah corrected him for the hundredth time. "You don't shout 'fire' on a boat."

I grinned. Things had been "cool" or "not cool" for almost a hundred years and the word had transcended generations. What was cool in the fifties would have been considered outlandish when the term was first coined, and would be tame by today's standards, and what was cool in the eighties would have been over the top by fifties standards.

Cool changes. But today's youth wanted their own version of "cool" and had chosen the opposite—fire.

Savannah's and my daughter Flo and her husband David were seniors at UF and were getting ready to build a house on Grassy Key. My oldest daughter, Eve, and her family lived in Miami and my youngest, Kim, and her husband lived in Everglades City but were also planning to build a house in the Middle Keys one day.

"What's under the seats? More storage?" Savannah asked, noting the hinge in front, and trying to pull the middle section open. "It's stuck."

"That's the kite sail locker Jesse mentioned," Hank said, pushing another button on the fob. Savannah jumped back as the three middle seats opened as one, like a giant clamshell, revealing the kite system below.

"Winds aloft are much greater than on the surface," Hank

continued. "This 130-square-foot kite system is push-button and computer-controlled, from launch to retrieval, and will fly far above where any mast-mounted sail can reach. If our calculations are correct, it should enable this *motor* vessel to travel at three or four knots in total silence with all mechanical propulsion turned off, when surface wind speeds will have *sailing* vessels traveling on *engine* power."

"Really?" Savannah asked. "How far off the wind would it be able to... what? Tow the boat?"

"Kite sailing," Hank said. "Or just sailing—the kite is simply a very tall, downwind sail. So, not much off direct downwind... perhaps eight or ten degrees for maximim power. Beyond fifteen degrees, the drag will put too much stress on the kite. It's recommended that it be flown only within ten degrees of dead downwind."

"Multiple sources of power," I said. "If it's a cloudy day and we're following the old trade routes, chasing the wind, rather than run the generator to power the electric motors, we can kite sail and the props will turn hydrogenerators to recharge the batteries."

Savannah and Alberto went to the office to look at dozens of paint, trim, and hardware samples, while Hank and I stepped up onto the soon-to-be sun pad to look at the exposed wiring, plumbing, and cabling that would be below the flybridge deck once it was lowered into place.

The structural framework of the deck was aluminum, just like the rest of the house, and the straight runs of wires, cables, and tubing through multiple two-inch holes looked like the framework of a modern airplane.

I could see the outline of conveniently located access hatches in the salon's overhead, near components that might need servicing,

141

and we'd designed similar hatches in the deck of the flybridge, giving even more access. Everything ran straight, clamped in place with even spacing between everything—miles and miles of it.

"Every wire, cable, and hose is marked every foot," Hank said, pointing to some of the nearer ones. "Any rewiring or replumbing will be child's play."

Hank and I spent the next hour going over minor details of the next phase of the build—putting the roof cap and flybridge on. Like the amas, the roof and attached flybridge, lounge, and outdoor grilling area were being built in another part of the facility as a single unit and it was scheduled to be joined to the main deck's overhead the following month.

Leaving it off allowed the techs to run all those neatly arranged miles of wiring and control cables more easily.

Finally, it was lunchtime, so we said our goodbyes to Hank, and the driver of the town car took us to a nearby hotel where we were going to stay. We had plans to see the flybridge in the afternoon, and tomorrow morning, Hank and I were going to dig deeper into the boat's mechanicals and review the final plans for launching her early next year.

Just as we were pulling under the hotel's portico, my phone chirped and vibrated in my pocket.

It was Rusty.

"I gotta get back to Marathon," he said when I answered. I could hear the anger rising in his voice. "Billy's gonna fly me back in his plane."

"Wait. What's going on?"

"That guy from Wyomin' showed up at the bar," he replied. "Sid had to call the law, but the guy left 'fore they got there."

"Stay where you are," I said, then lowered the phone and leaned over the front seat to tap the driver's shoulder. "Change of plans. Head to the airport, please."

"What's going on?" Savannah asked, worried.

I held up a finger to her as I put the phone back to my ear, and the driver pulled back out onto the street. "Slow down and tell me what happened, Rusty."

"Madison wasn't there," he said, "Happened 'bout an hour ago, right after she left to go to the Publix. She still ain't back yet. But Sid could tell by the way the guy looked, talked, and carried himself that it was him. He asked about Madison, givin' Sid a fake name, and sayin' he'd run into her down in Key Weird."

"And, of course, Sid called him on it," I said, knowing she wasn't one to mince words.

"She did," Rusty affirmed. "Then she called the law, and he started bustin' up the joint. She said he broke a coupla chairs and busted out a window before she pulled out the deck sweeper and he got to leavin' in a hurry."

The deck sweeper he was talking about was a sawed-off 12-gauge pump-action shotgun, with the butt cut off and the handle fashioned like a pistol grip. Rusty kept it behind the bar in a holster his dad made.

"I'll be there in a little over an hour," I told him. "No need for Billy to fly you down."

"Come straight to the Anchor if you're serious," Rusty said. "Me, Jimmy, Naomi, and Billy are already at the airstrip. Trish Osceola's comin' too."

I thought about just letting Rusty take care of whatever the problem was. He was capable enough. So was Billy.

Unless the guy had backup.

"Yeah," I said, deciding instantly. "We'll go straight there and be wheels down right behind you."

I ended the call and looked over at Savannah.

"The cowboy in the jungle?" she asked, dread in her voice. "No need to explain, I heard most of it."

"Looks like it," I replied. "Sid figured so anyway. She called the police, but he busted up the place, then disappeared before they got there."

"Called the police," Savannah muttered, shaking her head. "What happened to just calling friends, like Rusty always says?"

"It was late morning," I said, as the driver turned into the small airport. "About an hour ago. The half-day guides weren't back in yet, and nobody was around, except Sid and Rufus."

Rusty hadn't said as much, but I knew the ebb and flow of the people around the Anchor. If any locals had been there, they'd have come running.

"First that nasty little perv," Savannah said, shaking her head again, trying to keep her voice calm. "Now this." Her fists were balled up. "Rusty's family, Jesse. That makes Madison family, too, right?"

I nodded firmly as the car came to a stop. When Savannah had returned, we'd had a long talk about our future. She'd been afraid for me, but more afraid for Alberto, and what had happened in Marsh Harbor had rattled her. But not nearly as much as what she'd experienced in Mexico with Charity.

I was retired and I'd promised her I would no longer go looking for trouble or accepting *any* assignments or favors from Armstrong or anyone else, unless it involved family.

Savannah knew there'd be no stopping me if family was involved.

If anyone hurt someone I loved, they'd better hope that I died before I woke up.

Rusty *was* family. And that meant Madison was family, also.

We piled out, and the driver helped me unload the minimal baggage. "Tell Hank I'm sorry," I told him. "Let him know we had to get back in a hurry—a family emergency. I'll call and reschedule the rest for next week or the week after."

The door to the general aviation building opened as I was quickly loading our luggage back into the plane. The fuel man came out with a clipboard.

"Looks like you're in a hurry," he said. "I thought you were staying another day."

"An emergency came up at home," Savannah replied, before I could say anything. "Is that our gas receipt?"

As I removed the tie-downs, she took the clipboard from the man, removed my card from the top, and put it in her pocket. Then she signed the receipt and handed the clipboard back.

Ten minutes later, we were in the air and climbing over the sawgrass below. Savannah rode up front with me, but as soon as we were in the air, she was texting Sid.

I leveled off, and Savannah began giving me a play-by-play of her text messages.

As we reached the edge of the Glades and soared out over Florida Bay, Savannah's excited voice came over my headset. "She says the guy with the dogs was just at Publix!"

Oh no, I thought. "Madison?"

"*Yes*," she said coldly, and I could sense the anger in that one clipped syllable. "Oooh, give me ten minutes with that creep."

I glanced over at her. Savannah usually ran on a very even keel, and rarely became angry. Emotional? Yeah. Shut down? Absolutely. But she didn't allow anger to come out in front of others very often.

And right now, she was seething.

Forty minutes later, as we flew across Mac and Mel's island, with ours just under the starboard wing, I began banking to the left.

"Where are you going?" Savannah asked, as we approached Bahia Honda, having overshot the airport approach.

"He said come straight to the Anchor," I replied, pointing to the east. "There's Billy."

Though it was a good ten or eleven miles away, the amphibious plane I could see skimming across the water beyond the east end of the Seven Mile Bridge could only be Billy's. He flew an almost identical yellow deHavilland Beaver.

Fifteen minutes later, *Island Hopper* waddled up the boat ramp at the back of the Rusty Anchor as I gunned the engine. Billy had parked in the grass, so I turned right and brought the *Hopper* up next to his plane, then set the brakes and started through a quick shutdown.

I *knew* Savannah was going to go straight in, so I quickly unbuckled my harness while I shut off the fuel and batteries before climbing out of my seat and following her.

What I *didn't* know was if the guy might still be around.

CHAPTER EIGHTEEN

As we started across the yard, I heard the door to the old rum shack slam shut and turned to see Rufus coming after us at a trot. He was very old, though nobody knew exactly how old, and he'd been the chef of the Rusty Anchor for almost twenty years.

Rufus used to live in the little building that had once been a rum distillery, but he'd moved in with Rusty and Sid a few years ago, when his tiny house had been submerged by Irma.

I'd just assumed he'd continued to live in the house.

"Din know dere was a fly-in, Cap'n," he said, angling to join us and looking back at the two old planes.

"You're back to living in the old rum shack?" I asked him. "I know firsthand the view can be mesmerizing."

"Oh, no, Cap'n," he said, walking next to me and smiling. "I and I still livin' in di main house. Dem windows be perfec' fo' di ganja."

"Ganja?" I asked, low enough that Alberto couldn't hear.

"Fo' di joint pains," he said. "Jest wait to yuh get my age."

"How old are you, Rufus?" I asked bluntly.

Even Rusty had never asked the man his age.

He smiled, showing his bright white teeth with a gap between the front two. "Not t'ree digits yet, Cap'n. At least not dis time."

He turned away and headed toward the deck and his little open-air kitchen as we went toward the steps and the back door to the bar. If Rufus wanted to grow a little weed in the shack where Rusty's ancestors for several generations had made rum, that was up to him.

"What did he mean by 'not this time?'" Savannah asked.

"No telling with Rufus," I replied. "He sometimes says he can remember past lives."

"Like Jimmy?"

"Different," I said, taking the steps two at a time. "More ancient lives."

I went in first to find Rusty and the others gathered at the bar, along with the young deputy we met earlier and an older one, who I didn't recognize.

There were also two police dogs with them, both muzzled—a Rottweiler and a black Lab.

The cops were talking to Madison and the two dogs were sitting on their haunches behind them.

Rusty stepped toward us, and I asked, "Are those the two dogs that—"

"Take a gander outside, bro," he interrupted.

I looked out toward the parking lot and saw two sheriff's cruisers and another deputy. Next to him, sitting cross-legged with his hands cuffed behind his back, was the creep who'd talked ugly to Savannah and come a devil's whisker from becoming a greasy spot in the parking lot.

Rusty nudged me with his elbow and whispered, "Never fuck with a Thurman, bro."

"What'd you—"

"Wasn't me," he said with a grin. "Maddy took the guy down over at the Publix."

"You're kidding! She's shorter than you."

148

"It's that whole dynamite and small package thing," Sid said, joining us.

"Have the dogs had food or water?" Savannah asked, moving toward the bar.

Before I could react, she had a bowl from under the counter and was filling it with water.

"Excuse me, please," she said, trying to move past one of the deputies. "Those dogs need water."

"They can't drink while muzzled, ma'am."

"Remove the muzzles," Savannah said, and her tone was serious.

"Neither of us are dog handlers, ma'am."

"Then get out of my way," she ordered, and looked down at the Rottweiler. "*Steh! Gib laut!*"

Both dogs rose and barked once, heads up, eyes and ears alert, and their attention focused on Savannah.

She spoke their language.

"*Platz!*" she ordered them, and both dogs dropped to their bellies, just as they had when I'd ordered them down.

"Stand aside, Deputy," Savannah said, in a tone that conveyed that she was accustomed to people jumping to do her bidding. "Or better still, go and catch that psycho cowboy who's after Madison."

He moved and Savannah stepped around him, then knelt in front of the dogs. "Good babies," she said in a soft voice, putting the bowl down in front of them. "Are you thirsty?"

She gently reached out and rubbed the sides of the dogs' heads, then, in one easy motion, unsnapped both muzzles and pulled them away.

"*Trinkin,*" she whispered softly.

Savannah stood and turned around to face me. "The Lab is

149

female and she's pregnant."

"How can you...?" I looked down at the dog, who was drinking from the bowl as the Rott stood beside her. What I'd originally thought was a larger-than-usual black Lab was actually *rounder* in the middle than usual.

"Less than a month, I'd guess," she offered. "But definitely pregnant." She turned to the deputy who was listening. "What was the date of the kidnapping of these K-9 officers?"

"October seventh," he replied. "Less than four weeks ago. Um, who are you?"

"Savannah McDermitt," she replied. "Was she pregnant then?"

"I, um, I really don't know, ma'am."

The back door opened, and Rufus came in carrying a single plate, which he gave to Savannah. It was loaded with at least a pound of chicken, cut into bite-sized pieces, and seared to perfection.

"It been coolin' fo' five minutes, Miss Savannah."

She smiled and took the plate over to the dogs. "*Nimm futter?*"

The dogs could no longer help themselves and both tails— or rather, a tail and a stub—began wagging.

Savannah had two new friends.

She placed the plate in front of them and the male Rottweiler turned to face all the strangers gathered around as the female moved to the dish and began eating hungrily. The stance of the big black and brown dog left nothing to guess at.

There was a line, and nobody was going to cross it.

"I think we're going to need more chicken," Alberto said, squeezing between Savannah and the old chef. "She's eating for, like *ten.*"

Rufus turned as the back door opened and his niece and assistant chef, Kyndall, came in carrying a second plate piled with

150

chicken.

Savannah took the dish and placed it in front of the Rottweiler. "Are you the baby daddy then? Taking care of your wife? *Nimm futter.*"

The Rott sniffed the chicken, then started gobbling it up.

The older deputy, who, until now, had only been observing, turned back to Madison. "So, you say he *did* expose himself to you, Miss?"

My eyes cut to the turd-fondler sitting on the grass as my blood pressure kicked up a notch.

Madison nodded. "That's when I kicked him in the balls and borrowed his truck. I walked to the store, so I felt like he was offering me a ride."

The older cop, whose name tag read *Patterson,* grinned and turned to Savannah. "You know police dogs, ma'am?"

"We had two protection dogs," she replied. "They died this past year."

"Her Rottweiler was protection-trained," I said. "Some of his training rubbed off on my Lab over the years."

"McDermitt," he said, snapping a finger, then looking down at Alberto. "Your Lab saved you from a shark. At least that's the story I heard."

"He did," Alberto said, looking at the dogs, now licking their chops over empty dishes. "What's going to happen to the puppies?"

Just then, the front door opened, and a man came hurrying in, going straight to the dogs, who obviously recognized him.

"Diesel! Molly!" he said, kneeling down between them and getting chicken fat and dog slobber smeared all over his face.

Molly? I thought. I'd had a Lab named that long ago, before I joined the Corps.

He stood and pulled a handkerchief from his pocket, wiping his face. "Why did you remove the muzzles?" he asked the deputies.

"She did," the younger deputy said, looking at Savannah.

"They were hungry and thirsty," she replied, when the man turned to face her. "Was Molly pregnant before she was taken?"

"Preg... No, of course not. She's in training, not even old—"

"Yes, she is," Savannah said. "She's at least three weeks; her teets are just starting to swell."

"Her... Wait! She's only eleven months old."

"Plenty old enough for dogs," Savannah said. "I'm just glad she was rescued. Is Diesel the father?"

"No, he can't be," the man said, looking down at the Lab. "That's one thing I'm sure of. He's neutered. Diesel's officially retired from police work but helps me with the recruits. My name's Kennedy, Warren Kennedy. I'm a dog trainer for Miami-Dade PD and a few other jurisdictions around the state."

Savannah McDermitt," she said, and nodded at me. "My husband, Jesse."

He was older, maybe in his early fifties, with graying dark blond hair and a developing belly. A little shorter than me; he was probably under two hundred.

"I've heard of you," he said, just letting it hang there.

The older deputy put a hand on Madison's shoulder, moving her toward Kennedy and getting a scowl from her in return. "This is the young lady who recovered the dogs, Lieutenant. Madison Thurman, from Greybull, Wyoming."

"You're a long way from home, Miss Thurman," Kennedy said in a soft voice, extending a hand. "But I'm very grateful you were here."

She shook his hand and smiled. "I *live* here now."

"Well, thank you for helping to get them back," he said. "If there's anything I can ever do to help you with something, please just let me know."

Kennedy started to turn, but Madison put a hand on his arm. "He called you... Lieutenant?"

"Retired," Kennedy said, nodding toward the Rottweiler. "Diesel and I retired from the force the same day. Now I just work with dogs. No more gangsters and drug dealers."

"Do you...?" she paused, lowered her head slightly, and looked up at him almost sheepishly. "Never mind. That'd be asking too much."

If she was *acting* the shy type, it worked.

"Name it," Kennedy said. "I've been going crazy these last few weeks with them gone. Anything you want."

"Do you have any pull with the sheriff's department here?" she asked. "I don't think they're taking my complaint very seriously."

"We only responded to the report of a lewd assault, Lieutenant," Deputy Patterson said. "But Miss Thurman says there's a man here from back up in Wyoming who she thinks means trouble."

"Have you filed a complaint?" Kennedy asked her.

"I only just found out he was in town when I got back from Publix," Madison replied. "It's a long story, but he's creepy and I think he's dangerous."

Kennedy turned his head slightly toward the older deputy. "She'd have to do that at the sub-station, right?"

"Yes, sir," he replied. "That's what I was trying to explain when all these people showed up in airplanes."

"Airplanes?"

"I said it was a long story," Madison said. "But to cut it short, the perv outside flashed me, I kicked him in his flasher, borrowed his truck, and brought your dogs here. That's when my..." she turned to Sid. "My cousin-in-law?"

"Just cousin works, I think," Sid replied, then turned to the Lieutenant and drew a deep breath. "Maddy came here to start over after her mother passed, and to get away from a psycho. He followed her here, all the way from Wyoming. Just after she went to the store and had the run-in with the man who kidnapped your dogs, the guy from Wyoming came in here. I pretended I didn't know who he was talking about when he asked about Maddy, because she'd told us all about him. He became angry and broke a few things before I called 911. And now, here we are, a crazy man who flew two thousand miles to rape this poor girl, and he's on the loose out there."

"Rape?" Kennedy asked, confused.

"This'd be the *long* part of the story, LT," Rusty said. "A coupla hundred years long."

CHAPTER NINETEEN

The guy who'd stolen the dogs and then gone around terrorizing women was called Max Belinski, formerly of Cleveland, Ohio, but he'd been in Monroe County for at least a year and had a list of prior offenses up in Ohio, similar to what he'd been doing here—lewd behavior, looking in people's windows, and two sexual assault charges that were never prosecuted.

Three interstates come into the state of Florida—one from the west and two from the north—as well as a number of U.S. highways. On any given day, there are more than a thousand more people coming in than going out, and it continues incessantly. With over twenty-one million people in the state, and the population growing at an alarming rate, there was little of the real Florida left.

Even the shape of the state seems to indicate this, wide and welcoming at the top, narrowing below that, and bulging at the bottom.

Often the dregs of society find their way all the way to the southern end of the state, following the two-lane ribbon of asphalt connecting the hundred-mile-long chain of islands—U.S. Highway 1. It begins in Key West and runs all the way up to the Canadian border in Maine.

After the cops hauled Belinski away, I appraised Madison a bit differently. It was one thing for a girl her size to ignore two barking dogs. But to go after an attacker who was quite a bit larger?

"That was a gutsy thing you did," I told her and meant it. "But what you should have done was run the other way and yell for help."

She took the pot from the warmer and refilled my mug. "With all due respect, where I come from, only coyotes turn tail and run. I can take care of myself."

"Oh?" I said, bringing the mug to my lips.

"Second degree black belt," she replied, almost demurely. "Tae Kwon Do."

"And what strikes would you use against two dogs that each outweigh you, have claws and fangs, and are police-trained?"

She smiled. "I remembered what Rusty said you did—I yelled '*Platz!*' at the dogs with one step, and 'Planters!' at the jerk with the next."

"Planters nuts," Savannah said, giggling. "I think you're going to fit in just fine here, Madison."

"I've decided I like Maddy," she replied. "Madison Thurman was a ranch owner and a cowgirl. Maddy's more of a laid-back island girl."

"Then Maddy it is," Savannah said. "At least that lieutenant was able to lean on the two deputies to take your complaint without having to go to the station. He seemed to take you seriously."

"The problem they have is in how the law is written," Billy said.

"How's 'at?" Rusty asked.

Billy shrugged one shoulder. "The man came here from hundreds of miles away, at great expense," Billy said, then turned to Madison. "He came here because of you. If that ain't a stalker, then I'm dead, and I'm still six feet. But Florida law defines a stalker as a person who willfully, maliciously, and *repeatedly* follows, harasses, or cyberstalks another person. It is a misdemeanor of the first degree."

"Are you a lawyer?" Madison, or Maddy, asked.

"This here's Billy Rainwater," Rusty said. "With all the commotion, y'all didn't meet. Me, Jesse, and him served together. And yeah, he's a bona fide Indian chief *and* a lawyer."

Billy extended a hand and they shook. "The keyword in this instance is *repeatedly*," he continued. "So far, it's just once here in the great state of Florida—what happened back home doesn't count here. If he comes around harassing you again, *then* they can pick him up. But even if he was in line at Dunkin' right in front of those two deputies right now, they can't charge him with stalking."

Billy's phone made a whip-poor-will call and he picked it up and looked at it. "Excuse me, I have to get this."

"I don't think someone coming all the way here from the northern Rockies is going to give up that easy," I said, then turned to Savannah. "I think we'll stay aboard *Sea Biscuit* tonight."

The exception would be in the case of family....

She nodded her head, then turned to Alberto. "Come and help me get the boat ready for the night?"

Naomi rose from her stool. "I'll go with you, too."

"We're staying here?" Alberto asked.

"It'll be dark soon," Savannah said, glancing at Billy. "And Uncle Billy and Trish are staying. He, Dad, and Rusty will want to catch up."

"No, we are—" Billy started to say, putting his phone away.

"We wouldn't want to put you out," Trish interrupted.

"Your boyfriend's family," Rusty said with finality. "And family don't get put out. We still have two spare bedrooms up at the house. The place was built for a multi-generational family. Lots of room."

That, I knew for sure. Rusty's house had been built for a large family, and had been added onto over the decades, usually after a hurricane, when they'd had to rebuild stronger. There were eight

157

beds in the house, and room for more.

Savannah and Alberto got up with Naomi, and Trish rose with them. "Mind if I join you, also?"

"And leave these Neanderthals unsupervised?" Savannah asked.

"I'm here," Madison said. "Go on. I'll see they don't get into trouble."

After the door closed Billy said, "Someone has been to my house."

I arched an eyebrow.

"My neighbor saw two white men parked on the road not long after we left," Billy explained. "Said they looked like cops. Short blond hair, not dressed right. He didn't think anything of it until he saw them again an hour later."

"You're not expecting visitors, I take it?" I asked.

He shook his head. "He said they left after he saw them the second time."

He showed me a grainy security camera photo. "This is zoomed in and a little distorted."

Judging by the three palm trees at the side of the dirt road, which I knew very well, the Toyota was parked about a hundred yards before Billy's driveway. Two men were in the front seat, both looking right at the camera. Though the picture was grainy, I knew I'd be able to recognize the two men if I saw them again.

Rusty turned to his cousin. "You didn't say nothin' 'bout that guy... showin' himself."

"I took care of it," Madison said, picking up a mug and absently wiping it with a towel, just as Rusty did when he was thinking. "And we got the dogs back."

Billy looked over at me. "Diesel and *Molly*."

My brow furrowed. "You caught that, huh?"

"What?" Jimmy asked, sitting quietly by the wall until the cops had left.

Though he no longer smoked pot, at least not that I knew of, he had an engrained shyness around the police, especially those with four legs, who could smell it on him after years of sobriety.

"Jesse had a black Lab when we were kids," Billy said. "Pap brought her home as a puppy not long after Bo and Helen died."

"Ahh," Rusty said, nodding in remembrance. "I recall meetin' her on our way down here a coupla times—once for the New Year, and again after we got back from Oki."

"I should have spent more time with them," I said aloud, without thinking.

After enlisting in the Corps, I saw my grandparents infrequently for short periods, usually on the way to somewhere else. Only when Mam's health was declining did I take an entire leave period to be with her.

"Who are Bo and Helen?" Madison asked.

"Jesse's folks," Rusty said. "His grandpa and grandma raised him from the time he was eight."

"Let's get back to the business at hand," I said and turned to Madison. "Just how dangerous do you think this guy is? Would he be alone or have others with him?"

"He has friends back home," Maddy replied. "Some, I guess. He paid another guy to follow me once. I know that for sure. I know he's part of some big, secret organization."

"Shriners?" Rusty asked. "Moose lodge? Somethin' like that?"

"Sort of," she replied, her eyes drifting up and to the left as she thought. "But not as outward. I know two other men in Greybull that I've seen him talking in whispers to."

"Rusty filled me in on the flight down," Billy said. "I would take this as a credible threat."

"He gave her the time frame he was plannin' to rape her," Rusty added. "I mean, yeah, that's crazy, right there. And crazy people been known to do stupid stuff—like kidnappin'."

"I'll take the late mid-watch," I said.

"Early mid," Billy replied.

"Since Rusty'll be up with the bar, I'll take last," Jimmy said. "Been getting up before the sun anyway, man."

"What're y'all talking about?" Madison asked, looking around at each of us.

"We don't turn and run where we come from either," Sid said, putting a protective arm around the much smaller woman. "There will be someone awake here all night. Nobody can reach the house without going right past the bar."

"The regular crowd should be comin' in," Rusty said, "and the guides'll be back before sunset. We'll get word around to the liveaboards here at the marina and over at Dockside. What's this guy look like?"

"His name's Marshall Grey," she said. "He's tall..." She looked up at me and Billy. "About halfway between you two."

"Six-one or six-two then," Rusty said.

"He's what we call rangy," she said. "Thin, but not bony. Built kind of like Jimmy."

"I'm six feet and one-eighty," he said, nodding. "And I've been called rangy before."

"So, about six-one and one-ninety," I said. "Hair? Face? Any tattoos or scars."

"No tats that I know of," she replied. "But he does have a scar on his chin, right here," she ran her index finger along her right jawbone. "He got kicked by a packhorse. He has kind of dark reddish-brown hair, usually slicked back and down to his shoulders."

"Facial hair?" Rusty asked, stroking his gray beard.

She shook her head.

"He wore jeans and cowboy boots when he came in," Sid added. "A western shirt, unbuttoned, and his sleeves rolled up, a plain white T-shirt or tank top under it."

The back door opened, and Dink came in. "Jesse! Jimmy!" he exclaimed when he saw us.

He took one step toward us. hooked the toe of his flipflop on a chair leg and stumbled, arms swinging as he came toward us, trying to regain his balance.

"This must be Dink," Madison said, smiling up at the man.

"Who are you?" Dink asked, puzzled, as he steadied himself on the bar with his right hand.

"My cousin, Maddy," Rusty said. "And yeah, this is the famous, or maybe *infamous*, backcountry guide, Dink Wilcox, dependin' on who ya talk to."

"I just gave Rufus two, whole, cleaned and gutted cobia, eighty-two pounds total. What's today's price?"

"Eight bucks a pound this week," Rusty replied, as I finished my coffee. "Keep 'em comin'. Sid's working on a way to ship overnight to customers online."

"Beer me," Dink said. "I'm fish-rich on a Friday night."

"What exactly did you guys do in the Marines?" Madison asked, looking around at the four of us.

"The Marine Corps has always been the sharp spear of America's military," Rusty said. "First to fight."

"And Force Recon," Billy added with a wink, "is the pointy tip of that spear."

"Not me, *chica*," Jimmy said. "I was a Navy ET—electronics tech—not the pointy tip, but without us, they wouldn't know which way to point it."

The back door opened, and Trish came back in with Savannah.

"Where's Alberto?" I asked, as more people came in the front door.

"He and Naomi are playing a video game," she replied.

Trish sat down next to Billy. "Did you assign watch?"

He nodded. "We have the early mid-watch, midnight to two."

"We?" I asked without thinking.

"You didn't know?" Savannah asked, sitting beside me.

"Know what?"

"Trish was in the Marines too," she replied.

"Linguistics," Trish replied. "I speak a couple of Arabic dialects, as well as Russian, French, German, Spanish, and, since our trip to South America, I've added a couple more Amerindian sub-sets I'm learning."

"We spent three months together in the Amazon," Billy said. "The tribal people accepted us more readily than the whites, and we lived among them, learning their language and their ways."

Trish smiled at Billy. "They were very impressed with Billy's tracking skills."

"We're gonna duck through the woods, man," Jimmy said, rising from his stool. "I'll round up Naomi and be back here at four. Want me to send Alberto up?"

"All y'all should turn in," Rusty said. "Me and Sid'll hold the fort down till closing time."

I drained my coffee, then leaned over the bar and placed the mug in the little sink behind it. "Right behind you, Jimmy."

Fort, I thought, rising from my stool. Good choice of words.

Trouble didn't come around the Rusty Anchor very often, but when it did, it was always met by overwhelming force.

Next to the Corps, this was the only other place I'd felt a sense of closeness and camaraderie.

CHAPTER TWENTY

"Hicks are hicks," Marshall said with a sigh, holding his cell phone up to his ear. "Doesn't matter if they're mountain hicks, bayou hicks, or island hicks."

"You overstepped in Louisiana, Marshall," the woman on the other end reminded him. "We can't have that kind of sloppiness and misguided intent again. There are generational issues at stake."

"I know, I know," Marshall replied. "But who's gonna miss her here? She only got here a few days ago. I can snatch her tonight and be back at the ranch by morning."

"We'd hoped she'd participate willingly," the woman said. "Her father and mother did, as did her grandparents and generations before them."

"Yeah, well, she doesn't seem to think like the rest of us," Grey said, irritation at the young woman he'd chased across the country evident in his voice.

"Your idea might have merit," the woman on the phone said. "Personally, I agree. But I'm not the one making the decision. It also depends on what she's told people there. Have you found out anything about any of them?"

"That's what's frustrating," Marshall said. "It's like nobody around here even knows what the place is called, let alone who runs it. There's no sign, not even a number on the mailbox. One guy I talked to told me a Playboy playmate was the bartender. But he was a drunk college kid from out of town."

"*You* are from out of town, Marshall."

"Tell me about it," he replied, looking through the rightfield fence at over a quarter mile of jagged shoreline, stunted mangroves, and salt marsh between him and the bar he'd been chased out of a few hours before.

"Watch and learn anything you can," she ordered, a faint clicking sound in the background as she typed. "But get some rest. We don't need you on a short fuse again. I'm sending the email now, asking permission to implement your plan, but if you don't hear from me by morning, check in first thing. Maybe I'll have an answer from the others then. Or they may say to do it right now. Just be patient."

Grey smiled but there was no joy in his expression. Rather, it was the smile of a prairie rattler preparing to strike.

He ended the call and put the phone back in his pocket.

The baseball field at the local high school was as close as he could get to the place without risking being seen.

The bar was surrounded by dense marshland. He'd probed the edges in a few secluded spots and found it'd be impossible to get through, except for the road going to it from the highway. And that was a quarter mile long, with no place to hide if a car came along.

No... getting in on foot from the highway would be too risky until the place closes, Grey thought.

If it did.

He'd been told that she'd been at that precise location for the majority of the last few days. Earlier, he'd simply driven in for a look around and had found that there was a restaurant and bar, as well as a house and several commercial-looking buildings.

He quickly realized that nature had rendered the place a miniature fortified compound. No barbed wire or even a fence to keep intruders out. Just the marsh and the tangled trees.

He'd looked around closely, noting the marsh on three sides and the ocean on the fourth. Going through the marsh on foot could be even more dangerous than the road. He'd heard about saltwater crocodiles in this part of Florida. Probably not as fast as a puma, but he wouldn't be able to see one until it chomped down on his thigh.

Certain that they got out-of-town visitors all the time, Grey had gone in and ordered a beer, then asked the bartender about the Thurman girl, just to get a reaction. She'd become cold and distant, putting his beer back without opening it.

The bartender had been a tall redhead in her forties or fifties. There was something in her posture or attitude, standing there behind the bar, that had warned him that she was armed. Whether it was a gun or a baseball bat didn't matter. She was nearly his size and he had nothing.

Another boat came out of the canal that ran up to the place, turned toward the big bridge and was soon out of sight.

Maybe I should steal a boat, he thought, looking out over the water.

A boat *would* make getting away with the girl easier, since the single lane road was too easily blocked.

If he knew anything at all about boats, which he didn't.

Marshall raised the binoculars again. He'd seen people coming and going, some leaving by car and some by boat. And even a few who lived on boats tied up at the place.

How the organization had found or tracked the girl, he didn't know or care. From the bartender's reaction alone, he knew the girl was there.

It had been his job to keep her on the ranch until the time was right—mid-February—and he'd failed. Now it was his job to confirm that the girl was there in Marathon, though it seemed the organization knew far more than he did.

Grey felt certain that being allowed the chance to redeem himself had been granted because of his lineage. But whether it had or not, he was going to make the most of it.

The organization hadn't needed to find a suitable father for over two hundred years, and internal records were being searched for the right one.

Nothing was digitized. The records of the organization were kept in ledgers that were themselves three hundred years old and stored in vaults. It was the only way to ensure bloodline continuity. Marshall's own lineage was in one of those volumes, *and* he was a candidate for the Thurman girl.

The biggest trouble with written documents over DNA testing and computer matching was time. Experts had to examine dozens of generations in probably hundreds of handwritten documents to make sure there was no crossover.

The problem with computer-assisted DNA searches was that *anyone*, at any *time*, could be looking over your cyber-shoulder. If the information of what the organization had been doing since colonial days got out, it would ruin everything.

Another car pulled out and disappeared into the jungle that led out to the highway, the sound disappearing soon after the lights.

He swung the glasses back to the bar.

There! I got you!

He locked the binoculars on two women exiting the bar and instantly recognized the little firecracker, Madison Thurman. The other was the Amazon redhead who'd leveled the shotgun at him.

Please! Call me now and say it's a go!

There were only three other cars in the parking lot and all three had been there earlier that morning. He knew he could slip in now and grab *both* women at gunpoint.

There was something tantalizing about the sight of the two women walking side by side—one tiny and the other a giantess.

The plane was waiting.

One call would be all that was needed for it to be ready to take off as soon as he got there.

Please call me now!

The brassy redhead had been almost as tall as Marshall and looked fit—solid curves. She was a lot older, but still well put together.

Besides, he owed her.

The two women walked past the side of the bar to a large house built at the back of the property. They went inside and Marshall watched as first a downstairs light came on, then a moment later, the two upstairs rooms, one after the other.

A host would allow a guest to go up the stairs first, Marshall figured, so the first of the second-floor lights was probably in Madison's room.

Was it some sort of hostel or something? Why would the owners take in a stranger? Did she get a job and it included housing, like a bunkhouse on a ranch?

Madison Thurman looked great in tight jeans, but she was still a mountain hick. The fact that she'd gravitate toward similar people down here didn't surprise Grey.

Both upstairs rooms had small balconies, but they weren't connected to each other, nor did either have stairs or a ladder to the ground.

No way out.

He looked back at the bar. Some of the lights were off. The right side had been lit up but was now dark. Two people left the back area, a man and woman, both dark-skinned. They walked back to the same house where Madison and the redhead were and just walked in like they owned the place.

Maybe they did.

Or maybe they were just employees, like the tall redhead.

Marshall hadn't found out anything other than the name of the joint, and that was only because he'd had the presence of mind to grab a menu from a table as he busted a chair over it. He pulled the folded paper out of his back pocket and looked at it.

Rusty Anchor Bar and Grill
Best blackened hogfish in the Keys.
Hard to find, harder to forget.

The last light in the bar winked off.

Grey stuffed the menu back in his pocket and checked his watch. It was just after midnight. He raised the binoculars, looking across the marshy shoreline. There was only a faint blue glow from inside, probably a bar sign or the antique jukebox he'd seen.

A moment later, a short, bald man with a white beard came out and he also went up to the house.

It had to be staff housing.

Or family-owned?

No, they wouldn't take in a stranger, and the bald guy and redhead definitely weren't related to the black couple.

Staff housing.

Marshall continued to look at the house and the bar. Then, not seeing anything, he started looking over the whole property, searching by moonlight for any sign of movement.

Two of the bigger boats docked in the canal had lights on but there wasn't anyone on the docks or walking around the grounds, and he didn't see anything moving on the boats.

He'd seen a man and woman go into another boat just after sunset, but they'd turned off the lights. The man had paused, his head snapping around when a car engine had started up. He was older, but looked dangerous just the same. He hadn't seen either of them since they'd boarded the boat.

Not seeing anything, Grey lowered the binoculars slowly but continued to watch, satisfied that everyone who lived, or maybe worked there, was settling in for the night. A minute after the bald guy went into the house, the top right window lit up again, but dimmer.

He'd been right. Madison was in the room at the left corner of the second floor.

February was only three months away. He doubted things here would be any different. But by then, the Bighorn Basin would be covered in a blanket of snow that was measured in feet.

He and Madison would be alone in the snow-covered ranch house.

Grey smiled in the darkness, watching the house until the upstairs lights went off. He looked back to where the rental car was parked, hidden from the road by one of those portable classrooms. He could see the house from there and the bugs were starting to get to him again.

He'd sprayed himself down when he'd gotten out of the car. But even though it was November, he was sweating in the heat, and the stuff was wearing off.

Walking back toward the car, Grey thought about what was to

come. The wheels had been set in motion long ago and nothing could stop it. The list of candidates would be scrutinized until there was only one. They had to be close—they'd known it was coming for over twenty years.

Opening the car door, he reached into the side pocket and grabbed the bug spray, dousing himself once more. After putting it back, he closed the door, then turned and brought the binoculars up again.

Yeah, I can see fine from here.

Grey got in the rental car and put the field glasses on the dash, so he could dig his phone out to try and find out anything more. Every few minutes, he stopped and picked up the binoculars, but nothing changed.

He was tired. The long flight from Wyoming, coupled with the extreme change in weather conditions, was slowly wearing him down.

He tried a different entry in the search engine, and while opening one result after another, scrolling, then changing the search terms, his head nodded, and he soon drifted off to sleep.

The phone's display was face up on Grey's lap and the top search result read, *www.rustyanchorbar.com - Rusty Anchor Bar & Grill, Rusty and Sidney Thurman, proprietors.*

But Grey's eyes were closed.

The phone fell dark, and the only sound was Grey's snoring.

Suddenly, the sound of gunfire erupted, jerking him awake.

"What the hell?"

Grey picked up his phone, swiped the search engine clear, and checked the time.

He'd been asleep for over an hour.

CHAPTER TWENTY-ONE

I knew every inch of Rusty's property like the back of my hand, as I did most of the people who visited. It was set back from the road and, with its natural wetland "moat" surrounding it, the Rusty Anchor and Rusty's house really were like a fort, in that there were only three ways to get in—by boat from the water, driving or walking down the crushed shell drive through the overhanging jungle, or doing a short hike on a twisting, raised footpath on the other side of the dock area. It led over to Sombrero Beach Road and Dockside.

The only way to get to the house at the back of the property was to go right past the bar.

The wetland area surrounding the property was about three feet deep at low tide. It rose and fell with the tide through a pair of concrete culverts below the footpath.

The muck at the bottom had a way of sucking the shoes off a person's feet, making it all but impenetrable.

There were several unmarked sandy paths, which were knee-deep in dark water, but if you didn't know where they were—certain landmarks in the dense foliage—then they were just sandbars. The submerged paths were used by Rusty, Jimmy, Rufus, Kyndall, and a never-ending group of volunteers, who maintained the wetland as it was before the islands were settled. In fact, it'd become a rite of passage for newcomers to work in the muck.

As well, the wetland afforded a rookery for a large number of wading birds, and the tangled roots of the mangroves provided a safe haven for juvenile fish.

More than anything, though, the Rusty Anchor was home. A place where friends and family gathered to talk about the events of the day or plan for tomorrow, just as they'd done there for generations before Rusty came along.

Time and change moved very slowly in the Keys.

My quick survey of the property, what could be seen through the windows, yielded nothing—no threats.

But my lizard brain was needling me that there was something amiss; I just couldn't put my finger on what it was.

Just the excitement...

Savannah and I said goodnight to Rusty and Sid, then walked with Jimmy around the end of the canal. Naomi was waiting by the path when we rounded Rusty's barge, and she and Jimmy peeled off and headed through the woods to her apartment.

I paused and glanced back toward the parking lot, certain that someone was watching us, but there wasn't anyone there.

A car started and backed out, headlights sweeping over the wood line at the end of the driveway entrance. Then it was swallowed by the darkness, taillights appearing and disappearing through the jungle.

I didn't recognize the car, but that wasn't new these days. The Anchor was becoming a "known" unknown dive bar.

Had the driver been watching us?

The feeling of being watched was one I took seriously, firmly believing that it's a leftover instinct we all have but most don't pay any attention to.

I chalked this one up to some sixth sense realizing the person was just walking toward, or getting into the car that'd just left and not actually watching us.

Later, as I soaked in the shower in *Sea Biscuit's* master stateroom, I quickly forgot all about it.

I dressed and went up to the salon to find Savannah sitting at the lower helm station, sipping coffee and staring out at the stars over the water.

"Wishing we could be out there somewhere?" I asked, hugging her from behind and inhaling the clean fragrance of soap and shampoo.

"I can't stop thinking about the boat," she replied softly. "It's going to be magnificent." She paused and glanced up at me for a second. "But actually, I was just sitting here watching for any boats coming in. I don't think this guy's going to give up easily either."

"I hate to point out the obvious," I said, "but you're thinking like an island girl. This guy's a mountain man. The odds of his coming here by boat are slim to none. I'd be less surprised if he rode in on a horse."

"I suppose you're right," she said. "And any boat that comes in would go right by us, anyway. I guess I'm just jumpy."

I hugged her again. "You know I can't turn away from this, right?"

She looked up at me again and held my arm. "I wouldn't ask. Not when it's someone we love. She and Rusty may be very distantly related, but I don't have any doubt that he'd protect her to the same extent he would Julie or Sid... or you."

I looked out over the water, illuminated only by the stars. The moon wouldn't be up until just after midnight, but the stars were enough to see by. Turning my head, I could see the shadowy outline of Billy's and my planes on the back lawn, hunkered down like a pair of cormorants drying their wings. Rusty's house and the large metal building were dark, and the lights from inside the bar cast oddly shaped rectangles of light on the side deck. The angled shutters blocked any direct light from spilling farther.

Turning more and looking through the salon, I could see the parking lot and the gaping maw of the unlit driveway.

If I were a sniper—and I'm not anymore—I would make my hide on *Sea Biscuit's* flybridge, docked where she was at the mouth of the canal. The entire property was visible from there. That is, at least the clear part of the property. The wetlands surrounding it covered a good thirty acres and were impenetrable to the naked eye, even in daylight, being fringed by thick mangroves. My night optics removed all the shadows, leaving no place to hide.

"Have you named the new boat?" Savannah asked, still looking at the open water over *Sea Biscuit's* bow.

"Named?" I said, turning back toward her.

The change from tactical to civilian happened almost instantaneously these days. There were times in my life when I didn't need to change, and now, I was mostly in civilian mode. It had been a necessity when I was a young father, husband, *and* Marine.

"No. No name yet," I replied. "I wanted to wait until we saw it coming together and get your input. We still have three or four months before we splash her for the first time."

"Where will we go?"

"The first time?" I asked. "The run down here from Stuart will be a good shakedown, then we can stock up, weigh anchor, and spend the summer in the Bahamas and never bump a dock."

"Not even in the tender?"

"You really *do* want to get away from it all," I said, pulling her

hand. "Come on, let's go to bed. I have to relieve Billy at zero two hundred."

"You mean *we* have to relieve Billy *and Trish*. You're not getting out of my sight."

"Jesse," Savannah softly whispered, touching my shoulder. My eyes opened before she said the words, "Wake up."

In one motion, I swung my legs over the side of the bed and stood up, remembering to dodge the overhead beam that'd clobbered me more than once.

"Someone's out there," she whispered.

It was a cool night, so we weren't running the air conditioning. Instead, we had the deck hatches open over Alberto's room in the forward V-berth, as well as in the salon, and the side portholes open in our aft stateroom. With a quarter mile of dense tropical foliage separating Rusty's place from the highway, the only sounds that could be heard would be from nearby—inside the treeline.

I went to the port side hatch and looked out as my hands found the knobs of the top drawer of the dresser below it.

Savannah came around the bunk and looked over my shoulder. "I heard whispers."

I looked at my watch in the moonlight streaming through the open portholes. The angle told me the moon was high—well past midnight—before my eyes even found the watch face.

It was 0143. The dead of night.

My phone vibrated on the dresser in front of me, Billy's name appearing in a faint blue light.

I touched the *Accept* button, then the speaker icon. "Savannah said she heard something."

"Three people," Billy said, his voice low. "Trish can see them better than me, but I could hear them halfway down the drive, coming on foot."

I quietly slid the dresser drawer open, and my hand went to the Colt 1911 I knew Savannah kept there.

I pulled the very familiar weapon out, press checked the slide, noting a .45 caliber round in the chamber, then double-checked that the hammer wasn't cocked and flipped the safety off.

"Stay here with Alberto," I said to Savannah as I started toward the door, phone in one hand and gun in the other. "Damn, I wish we had real coms."

"Wait!" Savannah whisper-shouted. "I can do this!" She grabbed her own phone from the charger. "Patch me in on your cell phone. Keep your volume low. I have starlight binoculars up on the flybridge."

I stopped and looked into her eyes in the moonlight. I'd read Charity's and Paul's after-action reports about the incident in the Yucatan. Savannah had been the eyes for an operation to rescue a kidnapped American college girl and had given the order to take a man's life. While it was Charity who'd actually pulled the trigger, Savannah carried a great deal of weight for giving the order.

I could see a touch of fear in her eyes but beyond that, I saw the resolve and courage born of battle that I'd seen in many warriors.

"Call me and give us a slow count," I said, then pulled my phone out and headed up to the salon.

I moved forward to the lower helm and accepted Savannah's call, putting all three of us on the same line. As she counted, I adjusted the volume so I could just hear her, then slipped the phone into my T-shirt pocket.

"Billy, I'm coming out the starboard side hatch," I said, slowly turning the latch.

"I'm on, too," Trish said, her voice barely audible.

"Are either of you armed?" Savannah asked. "Jesse has my 1911."

"Geez, Louise, Kemosabe. These aren't elephants."

"We're both armed," Trish added.

"First thing I grabbed," I replied, stepping up onto the side deck in a crouch, with Savannah right behind me. "Savvy's going up to the flybridge," I whispered. "She can direct us, using night optic binos."

"The moon's shining right on those mangroves just past your boat," Billy warned. "They're near the driveway. You'll be in the open all the way around. I suggest you swim over and use the bar to block them seeing you."

"Roger that," I whispered.

"Wait," Savannah said, and disappeared back inside.

She emerged a few seconds later and handed me a ziplocking freezer bag.

I nodded and slipped my phone into it, sealed it, and turned the volume up one notch.

I quietly lifted the teak rail, laying it back on itself, then went over the toe rail sideways, left foot first. I found the dock and crouched by the boat for a moment, listening, before moving silently toward *Sea Biscuit's* bow, away from the bar and parking lot.

"Be careful," Savannah whispered, as she slipped quietly up to the flybridge helm and got low, looking toward the stern.

I put the Colt in one cargo pocket and the improvised waterproof com device in the other, buttoning them closed. Then I slipped quietly into the water, using the boat's bow line.

Directly across from *Sea Biscuit* was a small sloop in the spot where I'd once docked *Salty Dog*, the sixty-eight-foot Formosa ketch I'd given to a local school for troubled kids.

I'd had to dive to the bottom of the canal there more than once to retrieve a tool or something that'd been dropped, so I knew where a large crack in the seawall was located that provided an easy step up to the dock.

I climbed up out of the water as quietly as I could, knowing that the bar blocked any view of my location unless someone moved out into the middle of the parking lot. I pulled the zip-locked phone out and slid it into my shirt pocket again, still in the bag, then pulled the Colt out and crouched in the shadows, looking around for anything out of the ordinary.

"I'm out of the water, by the sloop's bow."

"One is moving," Savannah said. "Male, no weapon I can see. He's east of the driveway now, moving in the shadows toward the house."

"I'm going out the back," Billy said. "I'll intercept at the northeast corner. Trish will stand ready at the front door."

"I'll cover your nine o'clock sector from the other corner," I said. "Give me sixty seconds. Any eyes on anyone else?"

"Two others," Savannah whispered. "Close together about fifteen feet to the west of the driveway. They're down the bank slightly and I can't tell if either is armed."

Her voice was calm and professional. Letting Billy and me know that she couldn't see any weapons didn't mean they weren't there. It only meant that we probably shouldn't shoot on sight.

Living in paradise wasn't always paradisical. Home invasions and burglaries happened quite often in the Keys. Crime didn't stop at the mainland.

I moved quickly toward the bar, seeing Billy coming out of the back and disappearing around the east side. I couldn't go *around* the side deck on the west, since it was visible from the driveway, so I went up the steps and made my way along the wall of shuttered windows. Inside, on one of the tables, a laptop screen glowed, illuminating a notepad and pen next to it.

When I reached the end of the deck, I saw Trish standing beside the door, looking out, a semi-auto handgun in the raised ready position.

I swung my legs over the rail one at a time, then dropped to the ground and hurried to the corner.

"I'm in place," I whispered.

"Me, too," Billy said.

"I can see the one guy through the door," Trish warned. "He's nearer to Jesse, in the shadows, and picking his way slowly."

"The other two are squatting and seem to be talking," Savannah advised, her voice taut but calm. "You should be able to see them—there's a light of some kind."

Just across the corner of the small parking lot, I could clearly see two people hunkered down in the wood line. One was holding an electronic device, which cast a faint blue glow on both their faces, and probably washed out the image Savannah was seeing through the night optics.

"Two men," I whispered softly, ducking back behind the corner again. "Light colored hair, slim, can't tell how tall—they're squatting down, looking at a phone or something."

I heard a twig snap and looked again. Both men's faces were turned away, looking in the direction where the third man had gone.

"Don't move," I heard Billy say over my phone and from around the corner.

His order was intended for all three of them to hear.

I knew instantly that Billy'd somehow moved ahead of the solo guy and gotten the drop on him. I'd seen Billy move through the woods like a ghost, leaving nothing but his visual presence to follow. No sound, no tracks, no broken twigs.

The two men across the parking lot rose together, one with a rifle.

"Gun!" Savannah shouted. "Take them down! Take them down right now!"

CHAPTER TWENTY-TWO

I fired a round with every footfall as I advanced steady and deliberately toward the two men, laying down suppressive fire.

I was beyond accurate range for the Colt, but that didn't matter. The big bore cannon bucking in my hands insured that neither of the two men would rise from their position.

One man jerked and spun and I knew I'd hit him, as he suddenly went down sideways.

A .45 caliber ACP round isn't fast, nor is the 1911 the most accurate handgun in the world. But if you hit a guy anywhere, even in the arm, the impact of the heavy caliber projectile will take him to the ground.

Bright headlights flooded the entrance to the parking lot, and a car came roaring down the drive, stopping at the edge of the opening.

I put the last two rounds from the mag between the car's headlights, trying to stop the engine, then the slide locked to the rear.

The two men jumped in the car, then the driver charged forward and spun a half donut in the parking lot before disappearing into the woods.

"What's going on?" Savannah shouted, her voice audible across the water as well.

"One tango down," Billy said. "The solo guy I snuck up on. They shot him up bad."

"Are you okay?" I asked, as lights came on inside Rusty's house.

"Yeah, I'm fine," Billy replied. "I was standing behind the guy when they started shooting."

"They drove off," I yelled at Rusty, as he came running down the path with a shotgun in his hands.

I heard the thump of bare feet on boards and looked across the canal to see Savannah running toward the end of the dock.

"What the hell happened?" Rusty asked. He looked quickly back toward the house. "Sounded like a whole fire team."

"Three intruders," I replied, removing the mag from the Colt and cursing myself for not grabbing another. "One's down, over there with Billy."

We went to where Billy stood over the body as Savannah and Trish joined us. The dead man was fair-haired also.

And he had a gun tucked in his waistband.

"Was the cowboy one of the two who got away, then?" Savannah asked.

"I don't think either of the two men who got away was Marshall Grey," I said. "They both had short blond hair. Madison said Grey had shoulder-length dark hair."

"You'd better call the police," Billy said to Rusty. "Others must've heard the shots."

I walked over to where the two men had hidden in ambush. Why had they shot the third man? Did they think he was Billy? I looked back to where Billy stood as Savannah approached. The moon was bright and there was no way they would have mistaken the dead man for Billy.

Did they kill one of their own to keep him from talking?

Their reactions had seemed clumsy and unsure. People in combat for the first time will often fire blindly, their minds unable to keep up with what their senses were telling them.

Finding a twig, I used it to pick up one of the brass rifle casings.

"Got a light?" I asked Savannah.

She turned on her cell phone's light and held it so I could look at the brass.

"Large caliber," Rusty said, looking over my shoulder. "Cops are on the way. Best not disturb nothin'."

"It's a .375 caliber," I said, noting the brand name around the centerfire primer. "Blaser Magnum." I looked over at Billy. "Lucky for you they were probably hollow points."

Had the rifleman had a smaller caliber rifle with jacketed rounds, the bullets could easily have torn through the dead man and hit Billy.

The sound of sirens could be heard, and we all turned to see flashing blue lights out on the bridge over Vaca Cut.

"Guns," Rusty said, holding out his left hand. "A shootout between these guys woke us all up."

I handed him Savannah's Colt, and Billy and Trish handed over theirs, then Rusty hurried back toward the house.

Sid opened the door and came out, meeting him halfway to take the guns inside and stash them.

Not that any of our guns would ballistically match the slugs in the dead man's body, but it would just be a waste of time for the police, as well as us.

The Rusty Anchor was almost always a quiet, peaceful place. Except when it wasn't. There *were* occasional altercations, but they rarely devolved into a physical fight and almost never a gun battle.

Not that there had *never* been gunfire at the Anchor. Just like tonight, by the time the police arrived, whatever altercation had occurred was already over when they got there.

The response time of a well-aimed bullet is much faster.

Still, I felt violated, somehow.

Looking back toward the corner where I had come out firing just minutes ago, Savannah was already policing up my brass, depositing the spent .45 caliber shells in her pocket.

"There was a shootout," Trish said, loud enough for us all to hear, "and we all came out to find this man dead and a car tearing away. Does anyone know this guy?"

"I've never seen him before," I said, and glanced up at Rusty.

The man had been shot multiple times in the chest and torso and his shirt was a bloody mess. He had close-cropped dark blond hair, no facial hair, and no visible scars. He looked to have been in his late twenties or early thirties, with a slight build and average height.

Rusty pointed a flashlight at the dead man's face and bent for a closer look. "Never seen him before."

He picked up a dead saw palmetto branch and broke the dried frond off. Turning it backward, he used the saw teeth on the edge of the branch to pull the man's gun out of his waistband.

"They ain't gonna buy a shootout if this guy didn't at least draw his gun," he said, then turned to Billy. "What the hell's a .375 Blaser?"

We all turned to face Billy, waiting.

He looked around at each of us. "What?"

I crossed my arms.

"Okay, okay," he said. "It's a popular and expensive European hunting rifle. But do you have to *assume* I know every gun in the world?"

"Let's move over there," I said, pointing toward the parking lot and heading toward it. "We shouldn't be standing over the body."

"And you shouldn't be wet," Savannah said, catching up. "Explain that."

I turned to say something when the first sheriff's cruiser came roaring out of the driveway and slid to a halt in the gravel lot.

"You did tell them the scene was secure?" I asked Rusty as the car door opened.

The last thing we needed was a hot-headed cop thinking there was an active shooter.

"Course I did," he whispered, as he approached the man. "Hey, Deputy. I'm Rusty Thurman, the owner."

"Yes, I know," a familiar voice replied, as the deputy strode toward us, silhouetted by the car's bright lights. "I was here earlier. Deputy Munson. Seems like the same bunch of people." He looked around at all of us. "Mr. McDermitt, why are you all wet?"

I opened my mouth to respond when a second cruiser pulled in with its lights flashing.

Several of the liveaboard folks started coming out of their boats, gathering on the dock and near the barge.

"Where's the body?" the second deputy asked, as he got out of his cruiser. I recognized him as the older cop who'd responded the evening before—Patterson.

"Right over here, near the bushes," Rusty said, leading the way, then pointing to his left. "The two who shot him were over there."

"How did you know there were two?" Deputy Patterson asked.

"It was either *two*," Rusty replied, "or it was one firing a large caliber rifle and a handgun at the same time."

Billy and I followed after them, and he leaned close and

185

whispered, "Blaser rifles are manufactured in Germany."

I glanced over at him for a second. Like me, I knew Billy didn't believe in coincidences. Hunting rifles weren't the weapon of choice in South Florida, especially for a criminal.

And an imported hunting rifle added another layer of expense the average gangbanger wouldn't consider.

Street gangs on the mainland were armed predominantly with stolen handguns, AR-style rifles, or even AKs. Hunting rifles were too slow and cumbersome for a fire fight.

Then there was the question: why would someone with a German hunting rifle be coming after Madison? Did Marshall Grey have others working for him?

What if the shooters had no connection to Grey at all? Maybe Madison wasn't the target.

A German rifle? A German submarine?

The powerful beams of two flashlights illuminated the dead man's face. "Do you know him, Mr. Thurman?"

"Never seen him before," Rusty replied. "He ain't from around here."

The older deputy looked up at Rusty. "You know everyone in this town?"

Rusty glanced at his name badge. "Patterson, huh? You're Lester Patterson's son, from down on Ramrod. Heard you became a cop up in Hotlanta—didn't know you were home. You favor your mom, Ida."

The deputy studied Rusty's face.

"If Rusty says that man wasn't from around here," I said, "you can pretty much take that to the bank."

"What about you, Mr. McDermitt?" Patterson asked, turning to face me. "Do you also know everyone in this town? Have you seen this man before?"

"Those I don't know, I can find out about in a hurry," I replied. "In *any* town. But no, I've never seen this man before."

"I've heard rumors to that effect," Patterson said, then turned and faced Billy and Trish. "You two were also here earlier. What are your names?"

Billy stepped forward. "William Rainwater, attorney, and chieftain of the Calusa People in Florida. This is my fiancée, Patricia Osceola, councilmember of the Seminole Nation in Florida."

Patterson entered the information in a rugged-looking electronic tablet, then looked around at all of us. "Did any of you see the actual shooting?"

I pointed toward the far end of the canal. "I was on the bow of our boat." I wanted to get ahead of the question I was sure was going to be asked again. "As soon as I heard the first shot, I looked this way and saw the muzzle flashes of two guns."

"What did you do?" Deputy Munson asked.

"I'm a combat veteran," I replied. "I was completely exposed, unarmed, and vulnerable. I took cover in the safest way possible. I jumped overboard."

CHAPTER TWENTY-THREE

It was 0400 before the ambulance left, and nearly sunrise before the cops finished taking statements from everyone, all corroborating what happened. Everyone besides me was asleep and was awakened by the gunfire.

Savannah had gone back to *Sea Biscuit* to check on Alberto and get me some dry clothes and a towel.

Jimmy and Naomi had shown up for the 0400 watch and they too were questioned, mostly about why they were coming through the woods to a bar so early in the morning. Jimmy easily deflected the question, not knowing that a shooting had taken place, and had told the deputy that they were going fishing.

"I think you're thinking the same thing I am," I said to Billy, after we went inside and gathered around the bar.

"What?" Madison asked, still obviously shaken.

"I don't think these men were here after you tonight," Billy said.

As everyone erupted in conversation, I went over to the table where Trish's laptop lay, still open. I picked up the notepad and read several notes that weren't in Billy's handwriting. They were all about different German U-boats.

Picking up the laptop, I carried it and the notepad back to the bar.

"Let me see that security camera photo from your house again," I said to Billy, then turned toward Trish. "How long were you doing research on German subs?"

"Most of the evening," she replied. "Billy and I found out that nearly all of Germany's submarines were recalled to the North Atlantic toward the end of the war, so we started searching for those that didn't return."

Billy handed me his phone with the picture on the screen. The two men in the car were the same two I'd seen hunkered down beside the driveway and thought they were looking at a cell phone or other device.

"It was a geo-tracker or something," I said to Savannah, then turned to Billy and handed his phone back. "The device the two shooters were looking at. They were the same two guys that were at your house earlier... er, yesterday."

"They were at your house?" Madison asked.

"Not long after we left, just after noon," Billy said, looking up at Jimmy. "You were searching the internet for the same thing while we were there."

"I still don't get it," Rusty said, looking over Jimmy's shoulder at Trish's laptop. "How could they find us through a computer? It ain't like tapping a phone."

"May I, *princessa?*" Jimmy asked Trish, pointing to the laptop.

"Let me," she said, giving him an odd look. "It uses facial recognition."

She moved her finger on the mouse pad to "wake" the computer, then turned it back to Jimmy, showing the latest search result she'd found.

"This is U-320," she said. "It only saw combat in one instance and was badly damaged by British aircraft in the English Channel.

The reports say it was scuttled and the sailors rowed to shore in lifeboats. Several of the officers, including the captain, were presumed lost at sea."

Jimmy pulled a flash drive from his pocket. "Mind if I install an app I created, *princessa?*"

"Why do you keep calling me that?"

Jimmy looked at her, surprised. "You don't know?"

"Know what?"

"In one of your past lives, you were a princess," Jimmy said matter-of-factly. "All this app does is give your computer encrypted access to my StarLink account. Nothing else."

"A prin..." Trish waved a hand. "Go ahead."

"Actually, it's easier to track a computer than a phone, dude," Jimmy said to Rusty, trying to insert the flash drive, then flipping it over to the other side. "Anytime you access the internet, you're connecting through a modem that has an internet provider, or IP address. It's just a series of numbers and periods, but it pinpoints the user's geographical location. In the case of the old dial-up days, you'd be assigned a different IP each time you signed on—whatever internet provider corridor your computer connected to the web with. But here, and at Billy's house up in LaBelle, we were connected via Bluetooth to his modem, which has a permanent IP address."

"Like Chyrel did," I said to Savannah, "when I went up to Virginia after my ex-wife's boyfriend's killer."

"The technology's gotten better since then," Jimmy said. "Where she was able to give you a geographical area of a couple square miles, now it's more like a couple hundred square meters.

"But they can't trace it now?" Trish asked.

"Not a chance, *princessa*," Jimmy replied, removing the flash drive from the laptop. "The encrypted app I just installed on your machine is one I created myself. It connects to my StarLink account, and the app forces an IP address change every five seconds, a dozen changes per minute, using random IP addresses all over the world wherever StarLink covers, and that's just about anywhere now."

"And that's how they found us?" Naomi asked.

"It's a possibility," I said. "We don't know anything at all except they came here from Billy's house, armed with a German-made hunting rifle."

"*Exactamundo*!" Jimmy said, interlocking his fingers and flexing them outward. "And they're interested in Billy's sub. Now comes the hard part. If we assume these guys are German—and I mean, why not, dude? I can start searching for people recently arriving who have German names. But I'll tell ya now, there will be a lot of them. Germans love the Keys, man."

"Discount families with kids," I said, leaning closer. "And couples traveling alone. I'd bet we're looking for three or more men traveling together."

"What are you searching?" Trish asked, moving in closer.

"Customs and Immigration," Jimmy replied, typing away. "As well as TSA."

"What if they didn't fly commercial?" she asked.

"Don't matter, *princessa*. Private planes, boats, cruise ships, all entries are recorded."

"How do you have access to that data? Do you work for TSA?"

"Jimmy's more of an... independent," Billy replied. "Not affiliated."

She watched as screen after screen came up while Jimmy continued entering data.

"You mean he's a computer hacker," Trish said. "Am I going to get in trouble for this?"

"That's such a harsh word," Billy said. "And no, you can trust Jimmy. He knows what he's doing."

"I'm in," Jimmy said, then began scrolling.

Trish stepped closer behind him. "What? That was fast."

Jimmy entered more information on the screen. "I'm setting incoming parameters to include all Florida ports of entry from O-town to Key West."

"What's O-town?" Madison whispered.

"Orlando," Rusty replied, then asked Jimmy, "Why so far north? If they came direct from Germany, they prolly came in through Miami."

Jimmy stopped scrolling. "Unless you arrive in a business jet. Right here. Three men and one woman, all German-sounding names. Entry declared at U.S. Customs and Border Protection at RSW."

"Got pictures?" I asked.

Jimmy's fingers danced across the keyboard, then four obvious passport photos appeared.

"What's RSW?" Madison asked.

Trish looked over at her. "Fort Myers International."

The names beneath the pictures were Karl Gerber, Lucas Gerber, Paul Schmidt, and Hanna Hoffman.

"That's the dead guy!" Rusty said, pointing at one of the pictures—Paul Schmidt.

Billy held his phone out for everyone to see the surveillance photo from his house's security system. "And the other two are the shooters."

He was right. "Good work, Jimmy," I said. "Now check two things. The tail number of the plane they arrived on and where they're from."

"Already pulling it up," he replied.

In seconds, Jimmy had the flight history of the plane up on the screen. It was currently at Marathon Airport.

Rusty pointed at the previous entries. "Left Havana yesterday evenin', landed in Nassau, cleared customs there, then flew to Fort Myers, and now here. It's them, no doubt about it. But now they're short one man. What were they doing in Cuba?" he asked, rhetorically.

"There might be a fifth person," Billy said, looking across at me.

I nodded. "Someone already here who likes hunting."

"All four are German citizens," Jimmy said. "Different towns, various jobs, but all living close to the coast."

"And close to where the U-320 was supposedly scuttled," I added.

CHAPTER TWENTY-FOUR

There had to be an accomplice. Someone already in the United States, and most likely somewhere near Fort Myers—someone who'd supplied the guns. It didn't take a rocket surgeon to guess they had gone armed to Billy's house first, not knowing we'd already left.

The two men who'd killed the third were after us, not Madison, and they'd come to the Rusty Anchor armed and willing to kill. The woman, Hanna Hoffman might have been driving the car, or the accomplice.

Though entry into the States was relatively easy for Europeans, they couldn't bring firearms into the country. Not even if they were here on an extended visa. Even a U.S. citizen wanting a rifle from Europe would have to have it shipped to a gun store in the States, and the purchaser would have to go through an extensive background check, just like any other law-abiding citizen.

That was the biggest flaw in American gun laws—they only applied to those who didn't actually break the law. Most guns used in crimes were stolen or bought illegally from a thief on a street corner for drug money. To expect the criminal, who habitually committed crimes against society, to obey more stringent gun laws was just plain dumb. The laws applied only to the average, law-abiding citizen.

"I could check gun stores for the ammo," Jimmy suggested. "It's an unusual caliber, but not all stores require ID to buy ammo."

Billy nodded. "Do it anyway. The Blaser is a very expensive rifle, up into five figures for a used one. A person who would go to all the trouble and expense to own one here strikes me as the flamboyant type."

"It'll take some time," Jimmy said, hunching over the laptop.

I turned to Trish and Billy. "What else were you able to find out about this U-320?"

Trish picked up her notepad and started thumbing through the pages. "Let's see... Here it is. A report from an English fighter group identifying the three-twenty by number, claiming to have strafed and bombed the sub in the North Sea." She flipped a couple of pages. "And here. Statements from surviving crew members who all said the captain and several officers stayed aboard to scuttle the sub, keeping one of the life rafts."

"Tell him about the captain," Billy said.

Trish flipped through a couple more pages. "Captain Hans Gerber was born... Oh, my God! Gerber! It didn't register earlier."

"So, those two who came here lookin' for trouble are related to the sub's captain?" Rusty asked.

"Grandsons, most likely," I replied, thinking of the age difference between me and Pap, who'd fought in that same war. "Both those men in the passport photos are younger than me."

"Why're these Gerber folks so dang important?" Rusty asked.

"Oh, yeah," Trish said, going back to her notes. "Captain Gerber was the son of a sort of land baron near a small farming village on the western Baltic Sea called Eutin. He was listed as missing in action after the war, along with the U-320's other officers, and was believed to have gone down with his ship."

"Remember, the crew made it back to Germany," Billy said. "Their statements were all the German admiralty had to go on, and they all said the captain intended to sink the submarine."

I nodded. "It would be his and his officers' responsibility to make sure the ship didn't fall into enemy hands."

"Captain Gerber was the nephew of a Gestapo general named Heinrich Kaiser," Trish continued. "The general was from Hamburg, not far from the coast on the North Sea. He was captured on his way to Venezuela trying to escape Germany in late 1945 and put on trial for war crimes."

"War crimes?" Madison asked. "What happened to him?"

"He was convicted and hanged," Billy replied. "It was well-known that he'd squirreled away over a hundred thousand marks in stolen gold, as well as many priceless jewelry pieces. The gold alone had been equal to about fifty thousand dollars."

"The gold was never recovered," Trish added.

Madison sat on a stool beside Billy. "That isn't very much. Not to be looking for it that long."

"Not today," Jimmy said, without looking up. "If I remember right, gold was about thirty-five dollars an ounce at the end of the war."

"So, we're talkin' about what?" Rusty asked. "Fifteen hundred troy ounces?"

I whistled softly. "Over a hundred pounds. Today, that'd be worth nearly three million dollars."

Rusty's cell phone rang, sounding like an old landline telephone, and when he looked at the screen, he smiled, then glanced up at Billy.

"Thurman," he said, after tapping the screen and putting the phone to his ear.

The sun was up, and we'd all been awake most of the night. I yawned, then Savannah did the same.

"That's great news, Bill," Rusty said. "How soon can it get here?"

I had no idea who Bill was, but I had a sneaking suspicion as to what he was sending Rusty, who listened a moment longer, then thanked the guy and ended the call.

"That was Bill Black," he said. "He's a salvor up on the Treasure Coast, and he's got a line on a caisson big enough for what we need. It'll arrive here by truck later this afternoon."

"This afternoon?" Billy asked. "I thought you said it would take weeks."

"Guess we got lucky," Rusty replied. "He's got access to an inflatable caisson that should go over the connin' tower of the sub easy enough. We're only talkin' four or five feet down to get the hatch dry."

"An inflatable caisson?" I asked.

"Yep," Rusty replied. "It ain't deep, so the pressure won't be so much. It's made of heavy canvas around a flexible bladder, and used mainly for working on large bridge pilings in shallow water. We put it around the top of the tower, pump water into it until it seals, then pump *out* the water trapped between the caisson and the sub."

"I don't like that idea at all," I said. "Once we pump the water out from around the conning tower, then what? If we open it up and can't reseal it, the sub will be flooded. And a temporary inflatable caisson won't last very long. Nor that steel rail around the forward part."

I had my doubts about it withholding just the water pressure. How could something like an inflatable kiddy pool possibly hold back the Everglades?

But an adventure was afoot. The idea of being the first to open

198

a submarine that'd been missing since before Pap came home from the war and married Mam was a rush. That the three of us were doing it together made it all the better.

"It's a start," Billy said. "We can see what we're up against and if we can't get in without cutting, we just remove the caisson and wait for something more permanent."

I shrugged. "When do you want to do it?"

"We won't need the barge and backhoe for this," Rusty said. "We can fly the caisson up there in one plane and the water pump and hoses in the other."

Billy looked over at me. "We have a lot of work to do. We'll need to remove the seats in both our planes. That is, if you want to do this tomorrow."

I knew the assumption Billy and Trish had made in their minds—I'd made the same one. The captain had never scuttled the sub, and he and the officers had somehow contacted his Gestapo uncle and they secretly repaired the sub to smuggle the gold out of Germany. They might have even faked how damaged the sub was to get rid of the crew.

The Gestapo general had never learned that his stolen treasure had been lost and he'd been going to join his grandson when he was arrested.

CHAPTER TWENTY-FIVE

Though we were all tired, the idea of a possible fortune in stolen Nazi gold just sitting out there in the Everglades for nearly eighty years brought focus and excitement to our little group of adventurers.

Jimmy didn't find any leads through his ammo search, but he did find that there were only two gun shops within fifty miles of Fort Myers that carried that particular rifle cartridge, so that was a start.

"Those men came for a reason," Billy said, his tone serious. "And they came armed for bear. That is a very serious rifle."

"Yeah, well, Jesse's got some pretty serious guns, too," Rusty offered. "Bigger'n that one."

Billy's head tilted to one side, like a faithful Lab's curious expression. "I know. I sold most of them to him."

Billy was right, though. Those men had come to the Rusty Anchor armed, and we had to assume willing to kill. But what was their reason? What were they so willing to protect to kill one of their own? Or was I seeing it that way because it's what I expected? The heat of battle does strange things to people.

We felt sure they'd tracked our location, both in Fort Myers and in Marathon, by Trish's laptop's IP address. Or more precisely, Billy's home Wi-Fi and the guest portal at the Rusty Anchor.

Then there was the wildcard—the "cowboy in the jungle." Grey came all the way from Wyoming, for what? Control of land that was already on the market with interested buyers? The whole firstborn son thing was bizarre, to say the least. How did he fit into all this?

Two forces aligned against us at the same time was more than coincidental. But there was nothing linking the two. At least not that we could find.

The old proverb came to my mind—the enemy of my enemy is my friend.

If these two forces knew about each other and found that we were their common "enemy," they might join forces. We knew a lot about the cowboy but almost nothing about those who had attacked in the middle of the night, besides their names and that they'd come to Fort Myers from Havana by way of The Bahamas. Their backgrounds, at least what we could see, were varied, and didn't seem to have a common link—engineering, education, sales, and construction.

Jimmy was unable to learn anything more about any of the four, including the guy in the morgue. With today's technology, a person having no background on the internet meant one of two things—someone either chose to remain very private, like myself, or carried fake identity, also like myself, on occasion.

Jimmy had Rusty's laptop on the bar, and he and Trish were both doing more research while Billy and I got to work on setting up our planes for cargo.

We'd had six people on board when we'd left Marathon, plus gear, but it was what *Island Hopper* was built to do. The deHavilland DHC-2 Beaver was one of the most versatile bush planes ever designed. Besides its short takeoff and landing abilities, which were legendary, it could be configured in numerous ways to land almost anywhere and had exceptional cargo or passenger layouts.

Fitted with oversized balloon tires, the Beaver could land in very rough terrain like the Australian Outback. The landing gear could be replaced with skis for landing on snow or ice, like the oil fields of Alaska. Or, like *Island Hopper*, they could be outfitted with floats for landing on the water. *Hopper's* floats were manufactured by WipAire and had retractable landing gear built into them, making it a true amphibian, just like her big sister, *Ocean Hopper*.

Inside, there could be comfortable seating for six passengers and plenty of room for luggage, or the seats could be removed, and the Beaver could carry more than a ton of cargo and a crew of two.

Island Hopper was primarily a charter plane, taking fishermen to remote areas in the backcountry and Florida Bay, and even up into the Everglades a few times. At least, that's what I told the IRS it was for.

I did fly charters on occasion, but both *Island Hopper* and her big sister, *Ocean Hopper*, were used more for personal travel these days.

With Rusty and Maddy's help, we had the seats out by early afternoon, and stored them in the left side of the big dry-stack boat storage building.

What Rusty had said was right. Maddy was small, but she was obviously no stranger to hard work, and was quite mechanically inclined. I guess it went with the territory, living in a place that was snowed in and cut off for a third of the year.

Billy and I would fly the equipment up, and of course, Rusty would go with us to set up the caisson. The cowboy, Marshall Grey, was never out of my mind as we worked. What if he returned while we were gone?

"What time's the truck coming?" I asked Rusty, placing one of my seats in the corner.

He placed another seat beside it and then checked his pocket watch as Maddy and Billy brought in two more.

"Not for at least an hour," he replied, sitting down in one of the Beaver's seats. "Longer, if traffic's bad in Miami."

"When is traffic ever *good* in Miami?" I asked.

"We should go to the airport and refuel," Billy said, looking over at Rusty's 1967 Fairlane. "How's the big block running?"

"No need for that," Rusty said, rising from the airplane seat and walking toward the bench. "I got a thousand gallons of av-gas in a tank down by the ramp." He motioned Billy toward his workbench. "Got a new five-ten rear gear from Strange Engineerin'."

"That'll get you down the track," Billy said, looking over the dozens of gears and parts spread out on the table. "But... why'd you take it apart?"

"To inspect everything," Rusty replied, as if that was a foregone conclusion. "This low a gear should get me a big hole-shot and more important, hit the big end right at the top of the power curve in fourth gear." He paused and looked up at Billy. "Whatta we do if we can't get that tin can open?"

"We abort the mission," I replied, heading for the door. "Objective unachieved. Remove the temporary caisson and wait for something permanent. Even then, it's just not possible to get it out of there."

"Unless we blow the dams," Rusty said, catching up. Billy and Maddy followed us toward the bar. "But the right ones for *our* needs. I got a line on a civil engineer who might be interested."

I stopped and regarded him skeptically. "A civil engineer who's interested in domestic terrorism as a hobby?"

"It can be done," Billy said, opening the bar's back door. "Trish and I have both studied the water flow patterns in the Glades, and I think we might have an idea."

"Wait," I said, entering after Billy. "You were doing *online* searches of particular flood control dams where the sub is located?"

"Oh, man," Jimmy moaned, looking up at us.

"Yeah— 'oh man,'" I repeated. "If the shooters from last night found us because we were doing online searches for the sub, they might have the technology to see what other searches we've done."

"I doubt anything we found would serve them," Billy replied. "None of the dams were anywhere close to the submarine's location."

"Really?" I asked, not liking this turn of events. "What if one of them is a civil engineer like Rusty's friend?"

Trish looked up from her laptop. "One of them was an engineer. But most of our research on water flow was from recorded history, handed down from generations before. They would have to be an engineer who can read the Seminole language."

"That'd be a real big co-inky-dink," Rusty said.

"Okay, so we're probably safe there." I looked out toward the docks, still feeling jittery "Where's Savannah?"

"Her and Alberto are out with Rufus," Jimmy replied.

The front door opened and a man stepped inside, removed a pair of sunglasses, and looked around.

Jimmy and Trish both closed their laptops as he approached.

"I got a delivery here for... Rusty Thurman," the man said, looking at his clipboard.

"That's me," Rusty said, checking his watch. "You're early."

"Sign here," he said, extending the clipboard. "Nobody told me to take my time. If I'm lucky, I might get back in time to load again. Where ya want the stuff?"

"Is it on a pallet?" Rusty asked, signing the bill of lading and

205

handing it back.

"Two pallets," the truck driver said, then looked down at his bill. "One's three hundred pounds and the other's four-fifty."

Rusty nodded at Maddy. "Go get the forklift."

She took off, and I followed Rusty and the driver out to the truck. The back door was rolled up and there were two covered pallets near the lift gate. Besides them and a hand-operated pallet jack, the truck was empty.

"Want me to put 'em on the ground?" the driver asked.

"No need," Rusty said, looking past the two pallets. "This your last stop?"

"Only stop," he replied, as the forklift came out of the open middle bay of the metal building. The driver looked over at it. "Whoa! That's a lot of forklift for these little pallets."

"Only one we got," Rusty replied.

Maddy approached the back of the truck, slowed, then adjusted the width of the forks before gently easing them under the first pallet.

The forks were over ten feet long, meant for lifting boats out of the water and putting them up on racks inside the building. Maddy got them under the first pallet until they extended a good four feet beyond it. She lifted it and backed up carefully before maneuvering the forklift to pick up the second one. With the first still on the forks, she lifted them both, and backed up a little before opening the door.

"Where do you want them?" she called down.

"Stage them between the planes," I replied, then looked over at Rusty. "We can go ahead and load everything up this afternoon for an early start."

He nodded, and she drove off.

I followed the forklift down the gently sloping backyard, and Billy came out the back door and joined me. Rusty trotted up behind us, folding a copy of the bill and sticking it in his back pocket.

"He only charged me for the shippin'," Rusty said, always excited to get a deal on anything.

"You know the man well?" Billy asked.

"Don't know him at all," Rusty replied. "Bill Black's a treasure hunter from up on the mainland. He's been working the 1715 wrecks up in Vero Beach and knows the guy in Lauderdale who owns this rig. He probably owed Bill a favor."

"And now *you* do." Billy said.

"Reckon so."

It only took a few minutes to uncover the equipment and determine what would go on which plane. Surprisingly, it was the pallet with the heavy canvas caisson that weighed the most. There was a large intake hose for the pump, which weighed nearly a hundred pounds, and it was on the same pallet, so moving it and the pump to one plane better balanced the two loads, but the caisson itself was still a good five hundred pounds.

The three of us wrestled the flexible caisson into Billy's plane, which was no easy task. I was starting to have doubts about how this was going to work.

The pump proved to be the most difficult to load. With no land on which to unload and run it, we had to position the pump near the rear door of my plane, so that most of the exhaust from the gas engine would be pulled out if there was any wind at all.

I wasn't crazy about running a gas-powered pump inside my plane, but we really didn't have a viable option.

Rusty came up with a small but powerful rechargeable fan. It could be mounted near the cockpit window to blow fresh air into the plane and force the exhaust out.

"Just how do you figure on getting this over the conning tower?" I asked Rusty. "Won't we need a crane?"

"I hope not," he replied. "We'll have to get the plane right alongside, though. We can plan on gettin' wet."

Suddenly, there was a commotion from inside the bar.

"Get out of here!" I heard Savannah scream.

With my nerves already on edge, Savannah's shout sent an instant impulse from my brain, and I was halfway up the hill when the back door opened, and Marshall Grey stumbled backward through it.

"I only wanted to talk!" Grey shouted through the open door.

His hand went behind his back, and the motion spurred me on.

Just as Grey's gun was coming out, I launched myself up the steps, planting my shoulder low against his left thigh and wrapping his legs in my arms.

In high school football, I was a running back and receiver mostly, but I also played defensive back when the opposing team was in an obvious passing situation. I really enjoyed the mayhem my younger two-hundred-pound body could cause in the opposing team's backfield when I had an unopposed ten-yard sprint for a head start. I'd added twenty pounds of lean muscle since then and was still in top physical condition.

So when my shoulder hit Grey's thigh, I know he felt it.

The roar of a shotgun from just inside the doorway was deafening as I took Grey down hard, causing him to lose his grip on the handgun he'd started to pull. It skittered across the deck, out of reach.

I rolled with him and came up with his shirt front in my left hand and without hesitating, I went on the attack.

It wasn't *just* Marshall Grey. It was the turd-fondler who stole the dogs. It was the Germans who'd come looking for trouble. It was Tony Paladin, Vlado Novak, and every bully I'd met all the way back to childhood.

Something inside me snapped, and Marshall Grey just happened to be the one in my grasp.

My first blow landed solidly on the side of Grey's head, and though his body went limp, I followed it up with two more punches.

Jimmy grabbed my right arm as I was drawing it back for a fourth.

"Stop, Skipper!" Jimmy yelled. "He's down, man!"

I froze and looked up. Savannah was standing in the doorway, smoke curling from the barrel of Rusty's sawed off 12-gauge.

She was holding it in a high ready position, the barrel pointing at the sky. There was a spent shotgun shell lying at her feet.

Had I just beat the crap out of a corpse?

No. The shotgun blast had come after I'd tackled Grey.

I looked the other way and saw several small holes in the sunshade over the stage, where a man was crouched, a guitar at his feet.

She'd missed.

CHAPTER
TWENTY-SIX

I looked up, expecting to see a look of shock on Savannah's face, but what I saw there was rage. "He was reaching for a gun!" she explained, fuming, as I rose and gripped the stock of the shotgun and pulled it from her.

"Yeah," I said softly. "But he's not armed anymore."

Sidney came up behind her and took the shotgun from me as Rusty and Billy came running up the steps.

"Are you okay?" I asked Savannah.

Billy knelt and checked Grey's neck for a pulse. "He's alive."

Rusty picked up Grey's gun and handed it to Sid. "We can add another Glock to the collection." Then he turned toward the guy on the stage. "You alright?"

The man stood, picked up his guitar, and grinned. "Yeah, still intact," he replied. "Is this the usual Saturday night opening act?"

"Sorry about that," Rusty said, extending a hand. "Rusty Thurman. I own the joint. We only got one rule here—no guns. Who're you?"

Sid came back out with Maddy following her. The younger woman kicked Grey's boot. "Is he dead?"

"No," Savannah assured her. "Jesse just beat him up."

"Whoa! Hold on," the guitar player objected, stepping off the stage. "I didn't have anything to do with this."

"This is Jesse Rice," Sid said, standing beside the man, and motioning toward me. "The tall one is Jesse McDermitt. His wife Savvy is who was doing the shooting."

"The police are on the way," Maddy said.

More introductions were made, and several more people came out onto the deck. Some barely noticed the unconscious man.

"What exactly is going on here?" Jesse Rice asked me.

"It's a long story," I replied.

"Aren't they all?"

"The cowboy layin' there on the deck," Rusty began, pointing at Grey, "came all the way from Wyoming to kidnap Maddy."

The younger woman stepped forward and extended a hand to the musician. "Maddy Thurman," she said. "I'm Rusty's cousin."

Just then, a sheriff's patrol car pulled into the parking lot for the third time in two days, and Deputy Patterson got out. Seeing all of us, he bypassed the front door and walked around to the deck as an ambulance pulled in and turned around.

"What happened?" he asked, coming up the steps and glancing at Grey. "Another body?"

"This one's alive," I replied. "Name's Marshall Grey."

"That's Grey with an E," Maddy added. "He's the guy I told you about."

Savannah stepped forward. "He came in here about ten minutes ago and grabbed Maddy, trying to force her to go with him."

"Anyone else see that happen?" Patterson asked, looking around.

"I did," Jesse said, stepping forward. "My name's Jesse Rice. I was setting up on stage and heard the commotion." He pointed at Grey. "That guy was being rough with the young lady here."

"Your first report's in the system," Deputy Patterson said to Maddy. "I think this qualifies as stalking now. If you'd like to press further charges of assault and attempted kidnapping, you really will have to come to the substation, and then to the courthouse."

"Add trespassin'," Rusty said. "My wife tossed him outta here yesterday and told him to never come back."

We made room as two paramedics carrying a stretcher came up the steps and began tending to Grey.

"How did he end up getting knocked out?" Patterson asked.

"He stumbled through the door," Jesse Rice said. "And did a face-plant on the floor." He grinned. "I should write that down."

Patterson looked around. "Anyone else corroborate that?"

"Yeah," Rusty said. "He fell flat on his face."

Several others nodded and mumbled in the affirmative.

Patterson took statements from the other witnesses as Savannah and I sat down at a table.

"You were trying to kill him," I whispered.

She looked up at me and took both my hands in hers. "You really should read *Prince of Tides*," she said, then looked down. "I won't lie. I wanted to. I was blind with rage. But a sawed-off shotgun loaded with bird shot wasn't going to kill a grown man."

A shotgun fires small lead or steel pellets loaded in a plastic shell casing. The pellets range in count and size from birdshot that holds up to five hundred tiny pellets, less than a millimeter in diameter, to just nine pellets measuring a third of an inch for buckshot. The longer the shotgun barrel, the closer the pellets remain to one another in flight. Sawing off the end of the barrel allows the pellets to spread out faster, making the weapon less deadly at longer range, but a lot easier to wield, especially when the butt is also removed, making it one formidable "deck sweeper."

Birdshot in a sawed-off would hurt, but it wouldn't kill. Not past eight or ten feet.

"How'd you know it was loaded with bird shot?" I asked her.

"I opened the breach as soon as I grabbed it, of course." She patted my hand. "I might not be a Marine, but I am a Southern girl."

Rusty and Maddy joined us, with Deputy Patterson right behind them. I stood and offered a chair to the deputy.

"Did your fist happen to do a... uh... face-plant also?" he asked me.

I looked at my right hand. The first knuckle on my middle and ring fingers were cut, though not bad enough to have bled much. I hadn't even noticed it.

"He hurt it loading the planes," Rusty said, a bit too defensively.

I held Patterson's gaze.

He was a local, though we'd never met. Rusty knew his father.

"I hit him," I admitted.

Patterson didn't even blink. "That changes things considerably."

"In what way?" Maddy asked. "The creep came here to force me to go back to Wyoming with him and have his baby next year."

Patterson blinked, then turned toward Maddy. "Have his... baby?"

"In the month of my twenty-fifth birthday," she replied. "I'll be twenty-four next week. His plan was to kidnap me, take me back to Wyoming, and then rape me every day of February."

Patterson looked around the deck area at all the people waiting to hear Jesse Rice play. The ambulance had left, and the place was filling up fast. Then he looked back at me.

"All these people were ready to submit false statements," he said. "To protect *you*, Mr. McDermitt." He paused and looked around again. "Why is that?"

I gazed around the deck also. Two tables over, Amy Huggins and her son, Danny, were talking to one of the fishing guides. The thirteen-year-old was animatedly describing a fish he'd caught, while his mother smiled brightly.

The boy's late father, Dan Huggins, Sr., had been killed in Ecuador when Amy was pregnant with Danny, and a man named Carmichael had stolen a fortune in emeralds from the house Dan and Amy had been building. I'd determined that her husband had gotten them legally and returned them to her.

Jimmy and Naomi were sitting with another couple, a young woman named Denise Montrose and a man I didn't recognize but had seen with Denise several times over the last year. Denise's father, a WWII hero named Kevin Montrose, had died in my arms—shot by a deranged musclehead while he was fishing.

There were others around us whom I'd interacted with or helped in some way over the years. During dire situations, like the aftermath of Hurricanes Wilma and Irma, these people pulled together and helped one another. I had the means and ability to help a lot of people, and never gave it a second thought.

My parents and grandparents had taught me at a very young age that money *wasn't* the root of all evil, as many often misquote from the Bible, leaving off the first four words from the passage in Timothy—For the love of.

A good person could do great things with money. Like helping a neighbor get back on their feet after a storm or accident.

Greed—the love of money—was at the root of all evil. Nearly all crimes, when you traced one reason to another, came down to love *or* money. Often, both.

I turned and met Patterson's gaze. "I can't speak for anyone but myself," I said. "But if you want, I'll change my statement. The outcome won't be any different, though. I was well within my rights."

Patterson looked down at his tablet, scrolling through several entries. "Stumbled out the door and did a face-plant on the floor," he read, then paused and glanced over at Jesse Rice, who was about to start.

"He was right," Patterson said. "It's lyrical." He looked around the table at the others. "That's what we'll go with, then."

To my surprise, Patterson rose, put his tablet in the cargo pocket of his utility trousers, turned to Maddy, and handed her a card.

"Your case number is on the back, Miss Thurman," he said. "Along with my phone number. I'm sorry your arrival here was marred in this way, but welcome to the Florida Keys. Please stop by the sub-station any time tomorrow and tell them you want to file further charges to that case number. I'm arresting him for attempted kidnapping."

"Then what?" she asked, looking up at the deputy.

"I'm not a lawyer," Patterson replied, his voice and eyes softening considerably. "I'm just a big city cop who came home to relax and cite speeders part time. But with the statements from you, Ms. McDermitt, and Ms. Thurman, I'd say the DA will have a slam dunk and he'll get at least ten years up in Raiford Prison, over two hundred miles upstate. I'd put my money on fifteen. Call me if you remember anything or just need to talk to someone."

Then he turned and walked down the steps, headed toward his patrol car.

Maddy was the first to speak. "That was a little weird." She looked across the table at me. "He's ignoring that you admitted hitting Marshall."

"In another place, in another time," Rusty said, as his eyes followed the deputy, "he prolly woulda done the same as Jesse."

"What do you mean?" Savannah asked.

"Les and Ida Patterson had *two* kids," Rusty said, turning back to the table. "Kyle there, and his sister Kara, three years older'n him. She went missin' oh, about fifteen years ago. She was nineteen then and her disappearance ain't never been solved."

On the stage, Jesse launched into his first song, strumming an upbeat tune I'd heard before—"Keepin' it Low Key." The crowd cheered and Maddy's eyes widened.

CHAPTER TWENTY-SEVEN

We stayed up later than I would have liked, listening to Jesse Rice play. Rusty figured nobody would be dumb enough to approach again if the place was open and didn't close up until midnight, even though we were all dragging.

But Savannah and I had managed to slip away to get a few hours of sleep before we woke and took the midwatch again, sitting in the bar.

It was highly doubtful that the shooters from the night before would return so soon, but we all felt it would be prudent to keep a watch just the same. The cops had less to go on than we did, and what we knew would be of no use to them without us divulging what we'd found out in the Glades.

"I understand how you feel, Jesse," Savannah whispered in the darkness. "And I understand that you have much greater capabilities than the average person. But I still worry sometimes."

We'd had this discussion numerous times before, and I really thought it was behind us. The violence that tended to come my way was what had driven her to run and hide last spring. And I'd vowed to avoid it in the future, mostly by staying hidden away on our island.

But something had happened while she'd been down in Mexico.

I got the story straight from Charity. Savannah's perspective on violence had been altered in a way that couldn't be undone.

Lately, it seemed as if every trip we made into town, there was some turd-fondler or other who needed to have their chain yanked, and yanked hard.

"We've already talked about it," I said, staring through the window into the darkness. "That's all behind me now."

"It shouldn't be," she said. "You should ask Deuce to give you some work—something you're good at."

I looked over at her, surprised. "I'm good at busting heads and killing people from half a mile away."

"Exactly," she replied, eyes glued to the window. "And you're intelligent. That's a rare combination in any man."

"I'll see if he has any despots that need to be gotten rid of."

She turned to face me. "I'm serious. I don't want you charging into the mountains of Venezuela, beating back cartel thugs. Nothing super- dangerous. But there are a lot of people who do bad things and go free just because of a technicality."

I studied her face for a moment, a little confused. The moon was rising over the water. Its soft glow had always been very kind to her.

"It sounds like you think I should be some sort of vigilante or something."

"If Alberto hadn't been there," she said, her voice soft but firm, "I would have cheered you on as you beat the snot out of that man with the dogs."

"No, you wouldn't have," I said, grinning, but confident.

She turned and looked out the window, seeing movement. It was Jimmy and Naomi coming around the end of the dock area, an hour early for the last watch.

"You're right," she said quietly, rising to her feet. "I would have gotten in at least one good kick."

Jimmy and Naomi came in through the back door as I got up.

"Go get some sleep, Skipper," Jimmy said. "You guys are flying in a few hours."

"What about you?" I asked.

"We're staying here, man. I think I can find those guys."

"How?" Savannah asked. "All we have are their names and pictures. They didn't go back to the airport, and none of the hotels have them as guests, Sidney already checked that."

"They gotta be somewhere, *chica*," Jimmy responded. "And sooner or later, one of them will call someone in the Fort Myers area."

He was right. They'd lost a man and whatever they were planning, their scheme had gone awry. They might contact whoever it was who'd armed them.

We left and returned to *Sea Biscuit*, going aboard as quietly as possible. Maddy had agreed to sleep on the sofa in the salon, so that Alberto wouldn't be left alone while we were on watch.

"It's not four o'clock, yet," Maddy murmured from the boat's darkened interior.

"Jimmy and Naomi came over early," Savannah whispered back. "Is everything okay?"

"He's been sound asleep since going to bed," she replied.

"And you?" I asked.

"I'm a light sleeper," she replied. "I heard you coming down the dock." She sat up in the dim light of the moon. "I've been thinking about that deputy," she said, pulling her knees up and wrapping her arms around them. "It's so sad what happened to his sister."

Rusty had told us the whole story while Jesse Rice had taken a break between sets.

Kara Patterson had left the Keys as soon as she finished high school and had been living in Atlanta for a year. She'd called her mother every evening after work, without fail, even on weekends. Then one day, she didn't call.

After a few weeks, her parents' repeated calls to the detective working the case were met with no further news and the case went cold.

When Kyle Patterson had finished high school, he'd gone to the police academy and then joined the Atlanta police department.

It didn't take a brain scientist to figure out why he'd chosen that city. What he'd said about being a semi-retired cop from the big city, coming home to work part-time, sounded almost like he'd given up.

Or maybe he'd found an answer to his sister's disappearance.

We said goodnight again and went to bed, sleeping until 0800, then joined the others on the deck for a breakfast of lobster and egg burritos.

Jimmy didn't need to hack into all the major cell phone companies to watch for a call from Marathon to Fort Myers—they all used the same cell towers. He'd stayed up all night, writing a code or application or something that would alert him whenever a call pinged off one of the towers in the Keys going to or coming from any phone number in the 239 or 941 area codes, which covered most of Southwest Florida.

By the time Rusty, Billy, and I got underway at 0900, Jimmy had gotten three alerts. It'd only taken a moment of listening into the conversation to know none of them were the people we wanted.

I was tempted to call Deuce and ask him to get Chyrel on it. But Jimmy was good, and he'd be insulted if I did.

We flew low and slow over the Gulf, just a few hundred feet

apart, and two thousand above the azure water. I was flying alone, and Rusty was with Billy in his plane.

I switched my headset over to the marine VHF radio that both Billy and I had installed in our planes and keyed the mic.

"How do you want to do this, Billy?" I asked. "Be a shame if either of us ran into that thing."

The idea of landing on the water, where we knew there was a solid, immovable object sticking up above the surface, was a bit disconcerting.

Billy's voice came over my headset, like he was sitting right next to me. "There's clear water just to the north of the pin. We can land west to east there, then taxi to the spot."

"I'll circle until you locate it," I said. "Pull up close and kick that donut out onto the top of the tower."

"Roger that," he replied. "We'll tie off with a hundred feet of line so you can get in close with the pump."

"Sounds like a plan," I replied.

I'd never heard of anyone ever trying to do what we had planned and neither had Rusty. And with his salvaging background, he'd seen or heard just about everything.

As we approached the coast a little north of Cape Sable, we spread out and I slowed down a little, allowing Billy to pull ahead to locate the pin on his phone's GPS.

"That's it," Rusty said over the radio. "I bet that clear area there was once a canal, too."

"I'll make a slow pass first," Billy said. "Hitting a big gator would be just as bad as hitting the wreck."

When he banked right and descended, I followed, but stayed at a thousand feet. I had a bird's-eye view of their perfect landing as I flew past and then circled high above.

I continued to make lazy circles as Billy turned his plane on the water, taxiing toward the south.

I spotted the submarine way before they did.

The water was dark, almost black, but knowing there was a sub down there and knowing what the dimensions of it would be made spotting it from the air almost easy.

It wasn't a distinct outline or anything, just a long, slender sort of shadow—a slight change in the color of the water. Seeing it made me wonder how it hadn't been discovered until now.

"It's off to your right a little," I said. "About three hundred yards."

"You can see it?" Rusty asked, his voice sounding surprised.

"Not exactly," I replied. "Knowing it's there makes it a little visible, but if I didn't know what to look for, I'd never be able to guess it was there."

Billy's plane turned toward the sub and I reduced power and added flaps, heading toward the same spot where he'd touched down.

A few minutes later, *Island Hopper* settled onto the water, and I throttled up to counter the increased drag trying to slow the plane, thereby keeping the floats up on top of the water. I gently steered toward Billy using only the foot pedals.

A hundred yards out, I reduced power and brought *Island Hopper* down off the step, taxiing slowly toward Billy's plane.

I wondered what a person might think if they looked down from a high-flying aircraft and saw two antique airplanes in the middle of the Everglades.

CHAPTER TWENTY-EIGHT

They'd only gone there to scare them. That was what Karl kept telling himself. It was almost like they'd been ambushed. As if the meddlers knew they were coming.

Shooting Paul had been an accident. When they'd arrived and found there were two houses on the property, Paul had volunteered to go to the one in back and check it out.

The building in front—Karl was certain it was a business and not somebody's home, along with all the boats docked along the wide canal leading to it— had altered their plan.

Karl had agreed with Paul that it would be better to check them quietly, and Karl and his younger brother had stayed near the road coming into the property, while Hanna waited in the car at the entrance.

The original plan was to determine how many were there, then simply breach the door loudly and overpower the occupants.

Karl looked around their Key West Airbnb. Hanna was on her computer and Lucas was sitting beside her, both talking in low voices.

Lucas had started firing wildly when they'd suddenly been attacked from two sides. He'd aimed at anything moving and began firing the handgun. Unfortunately, what was moving had been Paul.

"What's done is done," Hanna said, rising from the sofa where she'd been talking on the phone with their tech expert. "Manish knows two names and now has cell phone information for both of them. We must go back to Fort Myers immediately."

"What for?" Karl asked.

Since the shooting two nights before, he'd hardly slept. Finding his grandfather's submarine and the family treasure had been a driving force for most of his adult life—more than thirty years. Up till then, it had been piecing together clues and sometimes working in the hot sun. He'd never figured on being shot at. And now their cousin was dead.

"How they found grandfather's submarine doesn't matter," Hanna said. "But they *have* found it. I'm sure of it now."

Karl looked over at his cousin and younger brother. "The price is already too high. Do you want more family blood on your hands?"

"Don't be ridiculous," Lucas said. "Paul knew the risks. We were trying to warn *you*." He turned toward Hanna. "Pay no attention to my brother. What did Gupta find out?"

"The house in LaBelle is owned by a man named William Rainwater, Jr. and Manish is tracking his cell phone now. The owner of the place in Marathon..." She paused and looked at Karl. "Where our cousin was killed because you went in too fast, is a man named James Thurman and Manish is also tracking his cell phone. They are in the air now, heading back toward LaBelle."

"I told you those were airplanes I saw behind the building," Lucas said. "They probably have someone watching our plane up in Marathon and besides, by the time we get back up there, they will already be wherever they are going."

"Manish has already telephoned the pilot and told him to fly here to Key West," Hanna said. "If we hurry, it can reach LaBelle faster."

"And do what?" Karl asked, his voice rising.

"If they had airplanes in the backyard," Lucas said, "they have to be able to land on water. We just need a boat."

226

CHAPTER TWENTY-NINE

We were deep in the remote recesses of the Glades, far from any road or town. Billy and I somewhat knew the area and might even have paddled our canoes near where the sub was and never suspected it was there.

Of course, that had been decades ago, and the water was lower now. If the level dropped a few more feet, the sub would definitely be found.

There were signs of man's encroachment even this far back, if you knew what to look for. The Glades had been dredged, canals were dug and abandoned, literally crisscrossing the wetlands.

I felt pretty sure I'd just landed in one.

Billy's plane was tied up right alongside the exposed part of the conning tower. I turned and idled in a circle as the back door opened and Rusty appeared, waving.

I felt a bit of a shiver on the back of my neck. Rusty looked like he was having the time of his life, and I was happy for him—for all three of us. Billy's excitement level was up there, as well. He hadn't been acting like the stoic Calusa elder he usually was.

We were flying a pair of seventy-year-old aircraft and trying to unlock the secrets of an eighty-year-old submarine. Much like the things we'd pretended as kids.

A moment later, Rusty and Billy managed to wrestle the caisson out of the plane onto the highest part of the sub, barely a foot out of the water.

Then they both stepped over onto the sub and pushed the plane away, letting the light wind blowing across the Glades push it back out of the way.

Rusty let loops of line fall into the water one at a time as Billy's plane slowly drifted away. Finally, he tossed the rest of the line away and bent over to tie the bitter end to something on the sub.

Turning, I bumped the throttle up a little and moved *Island Hopper* toward them, approaching at an angle to make sure their line didn't get sucked up into my prop.

Still fifteen or twenty yards away, I killed the engine, opened my door and stepped out onto the portside float.

Opening the nose hatch, I pulled out a dock line and turned, throwing it toward Rusty, now just ten feet away.

He caught it and tied it to something on the opposite side from where Billy's plane was secured, then started pulling *Island Hopper* in close.

Billy stepped down onto the aft part of the float and took a second line from the rear storage, and Rusty secured it to the other end, where Billy's plane's line was tied.

The two lines were equal in length and on either side of the conning tower, so they'd keep *Island Hopper* turned perpendicular to it, above the aft part of the sub's hull. The tower was so low, neither man had to duck as *Hopper* turned and her wing passed over them.

"Okay," Rusty said, brushing his hands together. "We got you secured. Toss another line from the door and we can use it to pull the hoses across."

I climbed back into the cockpit, opened the side windows, and turned on the fan. Then I made my way to the back of the plane and opened the rear cargo door. I grabbed another dock line and tied one end to the intake hose, which was already connected to the pump.

"Will you guys be able to get the caisson over it," I called out, tossing the line to Billy, "or do you need me to swim over?"

Island Hopper had drifted, blown by the wind to the extent of the two dock lines, and there was a good twenty feet between us. Plenty of room for the high-pressure discharge hose to straighten out.

"I think we can get it," Rusty replied. "You can go ahead and rig up the other hose and get the pump ready."

While they worked on unfolding and spreading out the large canvas sleeve on top of the conning tower, I got busy with the discharge hose.

Both the intake and discharge were on the same side of the pump, so we'd secured it in place as close to the starboard side as possible to offset my weight in the pilot's seat. But because the discharge was three feet forward of the intake, we couldn't run both hoses through the door opening and keep them straight.

I'd seen what a high-pressure water hose could do and didn't want them widening my door frame, which was only two-and-a-half feet.

Securing the pump with the intake hose in line with the forward part of the door opening and the discharge in line with the back edge of the first window, I was able to open it and run the hose straight out.

"Make sure ya get it clear of the pontoon struts," Rusty said.

"It's a float," Billy corrected him. "Pontoons are on boats."

"Whatever," Rusty grumbled, as they flipped the last fold into the water. "I'm just sayin', when that pump goes on and the prime catches, that hose is gonna wanna straighten *right* out."

Rusty and Billy had first met at Camp Lejeune almost a year after Rusty and I graduated boot camp. Billy was in a different battalion, but his barracks wasn't far from ours. They'd become instant friends, though to hear them bicker constantly with one another, a stranger would never think that was the case.

Once I had it connected to the pump, I stepped out the door onto the float, and lifted the long discharge hose out of the water.

Billy had the suction hose rigged outside the caisson, and stood to throw me one end of the dock line he'd used to pull it over. I quickly tied it to the end of the second hose and he did the same, passing it on to Rusty.

"It'll take a while for the bottom of the caisson to sink," Rusty said, inserting the end of the discharge hose into a quick release cap on the caisson. "It was folded good, but there's still air in it that can't escape now. The weights at the bottom ain't much, and once it flexes all the way down, the air will keep the top floatin' on the surface."

"You have worked with one of these before?" Billy asked, looking around at the inflatable caisson.

"Nope. But I watched a coupla YouTube videos."

Little by little, the canvas sleeve fell down around the conning tower, disappearing into the dark water. Rusty and Billy moved around it, making sure nothing snagged. What air was trapped inside rose and floated the top of the sleeve on the surface, just a foot away from the tower, all the way around.

Finally, Rusty was satisfied and told me to start the pump.

"Be ready to shut it off when I give ya the signal, though," he said, making a slicing motion across his throat. "The air that's still inside will pressurize the water we pump in and give us a good seal down below the waterline, and under pressure, it'll be really rigid.

Enough for this shallow depth, at least."

I went back to the door, switched the ignition on, and pulled the starter cord. The engine started and there was a sucking sound as the air in the intake hose was pulled out.

When the water caught and the engine started lugging, the discharge hose flexed and straightened, jerking violently when an air bubble got sucked in. I kept my finger on the ignition switch, watching Rusty as the caisson began to expand.

It didn't take long for the pump and caisson to do their jobs and after just a few minutes, Rusty gave me the kill sign and I shut off the pump.

It was deafeningly quiet with the loud roar of the pump stilled. No bird sounds, and even the wind rustling the sawgrass seemed to yield to the silence.

The caisson was obviously made to be used on something round and that was the shape it tried to take, but because of the shape of the conning tower, it was held tight against it at the front rail and around the aft part, then bulged out on the sides.

I had my doubts about if it was even in contact down below, and if it wasn't, there was no way it would hold back the water.

Rusty released the discharge hose from the caisson's cap and quickly sealed it, dropping the hose into the water outside the canvas tube.

"I think this is gonna work," he said, always optimistic. "Billy, drop that suction hose down on that side and keep it close to the conning tower."

Billy lifted the intake hose out of the water where it'd been hanging and dropped it between the caisson and the side of the tower.

"All set," Rusty said. "Start her back up."

Again, I switched on the ignition and pulled the starter cord. The engine fired and instantly began pumping water out of one side of the caisson.

The water flowed from the other side, across the submerged part of the forward observation deck, until the level there reached the deck, exposing the hatch.

Rusty yelled something at Billy, who then pulled the hose out and handed it to him. Rusty dropped it quickly into the water on his side.

The pump engine revved as air was sucked into the hose, causing it to cavitate for a moment. Then it lugged again as water came rushing through the intake hose. The level on Rusty's side began to drop, exposing the upper five feet of the submarine for the first time in many decades.

Rusty made the kill sign again, and I shut off the engine.

"Watch it for a minute," I called out. "See if any water's going to seep back in."

Rusty dropped down onto the observation deck, peering over the rail at the water below. Then he moved to the other side, looking for any change in the water level inside the caisson.

"Looks good," he finally said. "But don't get too far away from that pump."

"What're you going to do?" I asked.

"What we came here for," Rusty replied, wiping the sweat from his bald head. "See if this thing can be opened."

He knelt and tried to turn the wheel to undog the hatch.

I moved away from the door toward the nose of the plane, where I could see what was going on.

"It moved!" Rusty exclaimed, and tried again.

Even I could see a slight turn of the wheel.

"Either of y'all got a crowbar?" Rusty asked, standing as more beads of sweat popped out on his head and face.

"Not standard aviation equipment," Billy said.

"Hang on," I replied, then climbed back into the plane.

In the rear storage compartment, I pulled out my toolbox and opened it. Grabbing a long ratchet extension and a big one-inch box wrench, I went back out onto the float.

"Do not drop these," I warned Billy.

He turned and planted his feet, ready.

I tossed the extension first, trying to keep it vertical for an easier catch. Billy snagged it and handed it down to Rusty. Then I tossed the wrench.

"The extension will fit through the box end of the wrench," I called out, when Billy caught it. "Added leverage. Want a hammer?"

"Let me try this," Rusty said, accepting the wrench from Billy, who jumped down to join him.

They were both on the lower portion of the conning tower and the aft part was higher, blocking my view. But by the sound of their grunts, I could tell they were both trying to force the wheel to turn.

From my vantage point on the front of the float, I could see the exposed side of the conning tower, down to about five feet below the top. Though dripping with mud and sediment, the tops of the numbers 320 were visible. Of course, it could have been 220, 330, or even 328, but I felt sure if we wiped a little more away, we'd find that Billy had indeed found the final resting place of the U-320.

Suddenly, there was a hollow clang, then a clatter, as one of the tools slid across the deck. That was followed by a splash.

"Don't tell me you dropped something," I moaned.

"S'okay," Rusty shouted, leaning around the tower and grinning. "It fell inside the caisson." His grin grew into a smile. "We got the hatch undogged."

"No way!" I exclaimed. "Can you get it open?"

"We'll know in a minute," he replied, then disappeared from sight, leaning over the rail. His hand came up, gripping the wrench. "Got it."

There were more grunts, and then a tapping sound.

"What's going on?" I shouted.

"The hinge seems stuck," Billy replied. "I'm tapping on it to get it to unstick."

There was another clang, deeper than the wrench or extension falling. It seemed to resonate through the conning tower.

"Oh, my God," Billy said, his voice low.

"What?" I shouted, about ready to dive in and swim over.

"It's open!" Billy replied, standing, and leaning out around the conning tower. "The hatch is open and it looks dry inside!"

"I'm gonna go down there and have a look," I heard Rusty say.

"Be careful," I yelled. "And Billy, keep an eye on the water inside the caisson. We don't want to swamp it now."

From twenty feet away, all I could do was wait. I stayed close to *Island Hopper's* door, in case they needed to pump water out again. The tension escalated with every passing second.

CHAPTER THIRTY

Rusty choosing to go into the sub wasn't a surprise. Submariners back then had height restrictions due to the cramped quarters, and he was more suited than Billy, who stood six inches taller.

After a few minutes, Rusty climbed up onto the observation deck and turned to face me. "Everything looks intact. No sign of any human remains."

"What do you think happened to them?" I called back.

He held up what looked like a leather-bound ledger. "Hopin' this might shed some light. Looks like the captain's logbook."

My satellite phone chirped an incoming message. When I pulled it out of my pocket, I saw that it was from Jimmy.

Inbound bogies, your pos, closing fast

"We got trouble!" I called out. "Coming in fast!"

Suddenly, there was a tinking sound of metal on metal, followed by a shriek. I recognized it instantly as a bullet ricocheting off the sub.

"What the—" Rusty started to say but was cut short by the report of a rifle.

"Airboat!" Billy shouted, crouching, as I stepped back to the door. I climbed quickly into my plane, seeing the airboat coming around a cypress head no more than a half mile away.

Hitting the conning tower with a rifle from that range was a lucky shot from a fast-moving airboat.

I opened a small storage compartment hidden in the deck between the forward seats, reached inside, and pulled out my own rifle—a Sig Sauer semi-automatic chambered for the .308 cartridge. It was loaded with match-grade Lapua ammunition.

Both Billy and Rusty had pulled handguns and taken cover on the observation deck, but their handguns were ineffective at that range, and they were hiding behind the inflatable caisson.

There was another ricochet and this one was followed by the hiss of escaping air.

"Close the hatch!" I yelled, then knelt behind the float strut and used it to help support the Sig.

I flipped off the lens covers for the optics and guessed the range and windage, then opened fire.

My rifle was zeroed at four hundred yards, and they weren't much farther than that when my first rounds found them. The man on the top jerked violently and the boat nearly went out of control, then another round hit the man with the rifle, and he slumped over. The driver on top started to turn, and the woman sitting beside the rifleman picked the weapon up and fired it.

My fifth round hit the gas tank.

The fuel exploded, sending the boat tumbling sideways as an orange and black fireball rose into the air.

For an instant, I saw three bodies flying through the air, splashing into the water with other debris.

It was over in a second. The Glades swallowed up the boat and it was gone, leaving a burning fuel can on the surface, part of a seat, and a black cloud rolling up into the sky.

Where Rusty and Billy stood, water began rushing in and the caisson began to collapse. There was now water spraying from the bullet hole, as the Everglades crushed in on the caisson.

"Water will always seek its own level," I remember Pap telling me, while showing me how to use a water level to keep the hull planks on both sides of a boat at exactly the same level.

Hundreds of square miles of the Everglades were pressing in on the caisson, pushing the water out of it and crushing it against the conning tower.

I rose, holding the rifle ready. "Tell me you got the hatch closed."

Rusty nodded. "How'd you know they was comin'?"

"Jimmy texted me."

"How'd he know?"

"I don't know, but I'm glad he did," I said. "I'm pretty sure that was the Gerber brothers and Hanna Hoffman."

"What do we do now?" Billy said. "Do you think there are others?"

"Might be," I said. "At any rate, unless you have a caisson patching kit, we're done here."

"What about the bodies?" Billy asked.

Rusty turned and looked out over the water, once more returned to its natural, peaceful beauty.

"Same as the other night," he said, then spat. "They come lookin' for a fight and got one. 'Cept this time, no cops. They're with their kin now."

He climbed up onto the back part of the conning tower and picked up the book he'd found.

"At least we got this," he said, as Billy joined him.

"And we know the submarine is intact," Billy added. "It may be salvageable."

I looked out toward where the airboat had blown up. I knew I'd hit the driver on top and he sat right in front of the tank. The man who'd been doing the shooting took a round in the chest and there was little chance of surviving that. But the woman...

"I think one might still be alive," I said.

CHAPTER THIRTY-ONE

A week after opening the sub, I took Savannah and Alberto shopping, and we stopped for lunch at the Rusty Anchor to catch up on the goings on in the Middle Keys.

We'd abandoned the ruined caisson and searched the area by taxiing our planes until we'd found the mutilated body of one of the attackers. A bar from the prop guard, or maybe the prop itself, had removed his head and right shoulder and arm. Nothing could be done for them, so after two hours we'd given up and left them to the gators.

We'd later found out that they were all related, the other two being cousins of the brothers, the last remaining grandchildren of Captain Hans Gerber.

The three German "tourists" who'd arrived in Marathon with the man who'd been shot, Paul Schmidt, were officially reported missing by friends back home who couldn't reach them.

They'd last been seen in Key West, where they'd been staying in an Airbnb on Caroline Street. They were wanted in connection with the shooting that had taken place at the Anchor.

When questioned by police, the pilot stated that the passengers he'd been hired to fly from Key West to LaBelle had never returned after asking him to wait, and when they hadn't called to hold him there another day, the aircraft was dispatched on another flight.

Rusty told us that Marshall Grey had been arraigned on attempted kidnapping charges, as well as a few smaller crimes, and was being held without bond at the Monroe County Detention Center in Key West, awaiting trial.

He also said that Max Belinski, the sleazeball who'd stolen the police dogs, was moved to Miami, where he too was awaiting trial—two counts of grand theft. The DA refused to press kidnapping charges for dogs. Apparently, not a dog-lover.

It was Maddy's birthday, and Rusty and Sid were throwing her a party a little later, so we decided to stay.

It was a day after Veterans Day and two days after the Marine Corps birthday, both of which I'd skipped this year. And Rusty's birthday was coming up in just four days.

Couldn't skip that.

"I got a replacement caisson coming," Rusty whispered over the bar to me. "And Billy and I are looking discreetly for possible ways to *legally* salvage the sub, since we know it's intact."

"Then why the new caisson?" Savannah asked. "You won't be able to do anything legally to get it out for some time, I'm sure. If it's even possible to get it out at all."

"Those last few entries in the captain's log," Rusty said, leaning over the bar. "Jimmy used an electronic translator gizmo and the captain had described how his remaining crew had tried to reach help, leaving in groups of two or three every couple of days, until it was just the captain and sonar man, with no food."

"But you didn't see any remains?" I asked.

"It ain't all that big," he said. "I checked everywhere a man could fit. They must have tried to get out, too. But it was the last entry that's got everything buzzin' in my head."

"What did it say?" Savannah asked, intrigued.

Rusty leaned close and whispered, "He wrote that his uncle's *legacy*—I'm guessin' that means the Gestapo general's stolen gold and jewelry—would *remain* aboard the ship until found and recovered by his heirs."

Maddy sat down next to Savannah. "I bought a house," she announced.

"You what?" Rusty exclaimed.

"I just got a call from my agent," Maddy replied, gushing with enthusiasm. "My offer was accepted. I have a condo overlooking the beach," She pointed out the window. "Right over there on Key Colony Beach."

"That's wonderful," Savannah said, as the door opened and a familiar face entered. "Now you need a boat to get back and forth—it's a lot faster than driving."

She turned and faced me and Savannah. "I want to thank you both for stepping in against Marshall the way you did. You could have been hurt."

"Say nothing of it," Savannah said. "We're both trained for it. And besides, we locals stick together."

I rose and put my hand out. "Lieutenant Kennedy, right?"

"You're a hard man to find, Mr. McDermitt."

"Have a seat," I offered. "And my friends just call me Jesse. Can I get you a beer?"

"No thanks," he said. "I'm driving. And please, it's just Warren."

"Coffee, then?" Rusty asked.

"Sure," Warren replied, taking a seat.

"How are Diesel and Molly?" Alberto asked, speaking for the first time.

He'd been quiet a lot lately, ever since he and Savannah had returned from Mexico. I knew he was sad about not being there to take care of Finn when he was sick.

"They're both fine," the police dog trainer replied, smiling at the boy. "Actually, I wanted to talk to you, too."

"Me?"

"About what?" Savannah asked.

"Well, while we had Molly in for a routine check, the lab took a blood sample from one of the pups in the womb. Just enough for DNA testing. When we got the results back, the department determined the pups would be unsuitable for K-9 training, and they will be adopted out."

Savannah and I both smiled. It'd been long enough, and we both knew it. We'd both had dogs around us for nearly our entire lives and the island seemed quiet and empty.

"What's that mean?" Alberto asked.

Kennedy smiled down at him. "It means that the department would like to offer you the pick of the litter for helping get them back safely."

He turned to Savannah. "I remember you saying you'd recently lost your two."

Alberto's head snapped around, and I could see it in his eyes.

"That would be so nice," Savannah said. "We will accept your offer on one condition."

"Condition?" he asked, sounding a bit puzzled.

"You let us pay for all of Molly's medical bills and sponsor the adoptions when the puppies are ready."

"There will be nine pups," Warren said. "And the father was a larger breed so Molly could have complications. The cost will easily be ten thousand dollars until their eighth week."

"We'd be happy to do it," I said. "Just out of curiosity, what

242

breed was the father?"

He looked me in the eye for a moment, then replied. "He was a Tibet mountain dog. I'm afraid the pups will easily be a hundred pounds when fully grown, probably one-twenty."

I grinned at Alberto. "A big dog like that deserves a big name to match."

He looked up at me. "What do you think about Tank?"

AFTERWORD

A lost German sub, deep in the Everglades? Is it possible?

I'd been toying with this idea for a while, researching information on Germany's U-boats during WWII, major hurricanes, and the historic water levels in Everglades National Park.

By comparison to modern submarines, Germany's U-boats were quite small, about a third the length of modern submarines and half the tonnage.

A modern, Ohio-class nuclear sub needs at least thirty-five feet of water when at the surface. The U-320 could operate fully submerged at that depth, needing only sixteen feet of water to float on the surface.

In 2005, Hurricane Katrina made landfall near New Orleans with a storm surge of 27.8 feet, the highest ever recorded in the United States. It washed over the low-lying areas, flooding the second and third floors of many homes and businesses.

But Katrina was nothing compared to Cyclone Mahina, which, in March of 1899, hit Queensland, Australia with a massive surge of 47.6 feet. Think about that—a wall of water that would completely submerge the roof of a four-story building.

So, yes, any ship with a sixteen-foot draft could easily be carried onshore by a storm producing a twenty-five-foot surge.

The barrier islands of Southwest Florida have an elevation of five to ten feet and the waters of the Everglades are barely above sea level. In addition, some of the barrier islands are separated by natural deep cuts. Before Flood Control, water in the Glades flowed unimpeded into the Gulf of Mexico all along Florida's southwest coast.

It would all come down to timing and location. I needed the sub to be going fast, barely submerged, trying to outrun a storm and find shelter in deep water when the water was actually getting shallower, so I broke the sub's compass, putting it off course by more than ninety degrees.

With a twenty-five-foot storm surge chasing him, the wind and waves at his stern, and the sub running at top speed just below the surface, the U-320's captain might have sailed right between two barrier islands and continued deep into the Everglades, riding the surge until the water receded.

As for the U-320, herself? Yes, she was a real German U-boat. And as I described herein, she was attacked by English fighter-bombers and severely damaged in her first contact with enemy forces in the English Channel on May 8, 1945. She was badly damaged and scuttled by her crew.

But I needed her to limp back into a port with a skeleton crew, get her repaired by wealthy relatives of the captain, and then put back to sea to smuggle stolen Nazi contraband, so that's what I did. She was fictionally repaired, only to be driven ashore after a comedy of errors on her captain's part.

The "rat lines" were real too. Toward the end of the war in Europe, and for a year afterward, high-ranking German military and civilian leaders attempted to escape Germany, mostly heading to South America, and yes, history tells us that quite a few U-boats were commandeered for the purpose of smuggling loot out of the country.

So, how much did Nazi Germany steal from its conquests? It's estimated that more than $200 million was looted from the conquered countries' vaults, private and public museums, individuals, and concentration camp prisoners.

Gold fillings in the mouths of Holocaust victims were removed.

That $220 million in 1945 would be worth $8 billion today. And that was just an estimate. Germany's total war chest during WWII was more than double that.

So, could a vintage WWII submarine be driven twelve miles into the Everglades with a fortune in gold aboard? Yes, I believe it's quite possible. And yes, German U-boat crewmembers did come ashore on the east coast of the United States. I read a report of a group of German submariners visiting Coney Island and riding the Ferris wheel.

On a more domestic note, I've been thinking about a new, four-legged companion for Jesse since early this year, when my family lost Kimmy, our thirteen-year-old Carolina dog. She was the last of three dogs we had all at once, for quite a few years. In the past five years, we lost Bill, age fourteen, Ginger, age fifteen, and then Kimmy, age thirteen. But for eight years, we enjoyed the sound of 48 claws clicking on the wood floors of our home.

Last winter, after we had to say our final goodbye to Kimmy, our home felt very empty—hollow. Greta and I have had at least one dog for all of our married life, and we both had dogs before we met.

We're dog people, just like Jesse and Savannah. So, after a couple of months, we decided to adopt a puppy.

Good Lord, what were we thinking? We're in our sixties.

Our puppy is a rescue mutt, obviously part dachshund, but no telling what else. I often wonder what breeds make up who and what she is, much like I wondered about our other dogs. We don't buy pets, have never owned a purebred anything, and never will.

Rescues make far better friends.

So, Jesse needed a pup. He'd had three good dogs, Finn, Pescador, and before him, Molly, who you have now met in *A Seller's Market*, the first book in the new Young Jesse McDermitt Tropical Adventure Series.

But what kind of puppy would suit Jesse and his lifestyle? A Lab like Molly or Finn? That's almost a given, as Labs love the water. But I wanted Jesse and Savannah's new pup to be a mix-breed.

The owner of the hair salon below my office got a puppy about the same time we got Milli. He's now eight months old and over one hundred pounds. He's a Tibet mountain dog and will probably top out around 120-150 pounds. Iggy—short for Ignacious—is the most docile, laid-back and gentle giant you could imagine. And why not? Simply due to his immense size, he has nothing to fear from anything or anyone.

Tibet mountain dogs were bred to protect sheep from wolf packs, not one-on-one encounters, and they were very good at their jobs.

Tank will be a black Lab and Tibet mountain dog mix, and he is going to be around a while—a stalwart and loyal protector, a strong swimmer, and bigger than many adults.

A four-footed Jesse.

I don't have to look far to find characteristics of a similar dog. I only have to remember playing with Bill, who was over a hundred pounds, could put his front paws on a man's shoulders, and could easily take down any intruder. A game of tug-of-war was only played after a complete liability waiver was signed. Bill was long-legged and powerful.

Molly, Pescador, Finn, and now Tank—four good dogs. By the way, Scott Kirby is real, too. He's appeared a couple of times in my books, and if you haven't listened to his music, why not start with "Four Good Dogs?"

Speaking of trop-rockers, I'd like to thank Jesse Rice for agreeing to appear as himself in this work. I contacted Jesse and asked if he'd like to play a fictional gig in a fictional bar in the Keys, for free. He quickly agreed, saying, "Yeah, man, I'll fictionally play Marathon any time!"

If you haven't heard Jesse Rice's music before, start with the Pirate *Sessions I* album. I just downloaded *Pirate Sessions V* last month and have been listening to it non-stop.

My recovery is continuing and going well. I'm back to walking in regular shoes up to a mile a day now. I couldn't have gotten through this without Greta. Especially in the early days, when I had to use crutches. I was unable to carry anything that didn't fit in my pockets. Just getting from point A to point B with a cup of coffee, required intermediate points C, D, E, and F while on crutches.

Greta brought me coffee, breakfast, lunch, drinks, snacks, and anything I needed. She cut the grass, ran errands, raked and burned the leaves and deadfalls, and looked after our growing puppy, all without complaint. She drove me to the eye doctor, the podiatrist, and anywhere I had to go until I was able to drive with the boot on. I've never had to rely so much on someone else. I love you to the stars and back, babe. It's Greta who deserves all the credit for this story, as well as *A Seller's Market*, being finished on time. Early, in fact.

By the time you read this, *A Seller's Market* will already be available in all formats. Just visit my website at www.waynestinnett. com for the latest releases and new preorders. And don't forget to subscribe to my newsletter. Subscribers are notified of new preorders at a deep discount, days before the price goes up and the rest of the world finds out. They also get a 10% discount code for use in my online store.

It's September 14 as I write this, fifty days after surgery, *Market* is ready to release now, and will be released any day, more than a month early. And this story is only waiting for Nick Sullivan to narrate it. But since we're both leaving this week to attend a writer's conference in Florida, recording will have to wait until the end of the month. But we did get *Market* done way early.

Thanks, Nick!

My team of advance readers and advisors are not only very familiar with my stories—they've read every one more than once—but also have far more knowledge than me when it comes to many technical things, and they make even the unbelievable seem legit. Thanks to Glenn Hibbert, Katy McKnight, Dana Vilhen, Mike Ramsey, Kim DeWitt, and Jason Hebert for all your valuable input and advice.

While at the NINC conference, Nick and I got to hang out with our favorite editor, Marsha Zinberg. She's edited the last fifteen or so books for me, and I think most of Nick's, and as always, she's done a stellar job finding quite a few inaccuracies here. I'm not just talking about typos and the commas I throw around like so much confetti, but plot points that a dozen or more people missed before her. The fact that she's less knowledgeable about nautical things, airplanes, and weapons is equally as important to me as her editing skills. Most of my readers are like her, and if she doesn't understand something, she lets me know.

Also as always, Donna Rich has the last critical eye on my manuscript, always finding dozens of subtle things that could be slightly altered to make the story read better. Why two to edit and proof? For the same reason an author shouldn't edit their own work. Marsha reads the entire manuscript several times in making her edits, and once a person knows the story, small mistakes can be overlooked. Donna's first read is a fresh set of eyes.

Thanks also to our kids, Nikki, Laura, Richard, and Jordan, as well as our grandkids, Kira, Lexi, Emily, and Jack. And lastly, our great-grandson, Kai. Your support during healthy times and convalescence has kept me going.

Don't forget to visit my Ship's Store, www.gaspars-revenge.com, established in 2015, by our daughter, Jordan. She has links to all the stores that sell my e-books, audiobooks, and signed paperbacks, as well as T-shirts, coffee mugs, stickers, and other swag related to my stories.

Lastly, if you enjoyed this story, the next one, Swift and Silent, will be coming in March 2024 and is on preorder until then.

Wayne

The Gaspar's Revenge Ship's Store is open.

There, you can purchase all kinds of swag
related to my books, and even my books themselves,
in whatever format you choose.
You can find it at
WWW.GASPARS-REVENGE.COM

Also by Wayne Stinnett

The Jerry Snyder Caribbean Mystery Series

Wayward Sons   Voudoo Child   Friends of the Devil

The Charity Styles Caribbean Thriller Series

Merciless Charity   Enduring Charity   Elusive Charity
Ruthless Charity   Vigilant Charity   Liable Charity
Reckless Charity   Lost Charity

The Young Jesse McDermitt Tropical Adventure Series

A Seller's Market   Bad Blood

The Jesse McDermitt Caribbean Adventure Series

Fallen Out   Rising Storm
Fallen Palm   Rising Fury   Steady As She Goes
Fallen Hunter   Rising Force   All Ahead Full
Fallen Pride   Rising Charity   Man Overboard
Fallen Mangrove   Rising Water   Cast Off
Fallen King   Rising Spirit   Fish On!
Fallen Honor   Rising Thunder   Weigh Anchor
Fallen Tide   Rising Warrior   Swift and Silent
Fallen Angel   Rising Moon
Fallen Hero   Rising Tide

Rainbows of Collars Motivational Series

Blue Collar to No Collar   No Collar to Tank Top

Made in United States
North Haven, CT
24 April 2024

51709399R00143